DAMASCUS

a novel by

Joshua Mohr

TWO DOLLAR RADIO
Books too loud to ignore

Praise for Joshua Mohr's
TERMITE PARADE

TERMITE PARADE TELLS THE STORY OF MIRED, the self-described "bastard daughter of a menage a trois between Fyodor Dostoyevsky, Sylvia Plath, and Eeyore." Mired catalogs her "museum of emotional failures," the latest entry to which is her boyfriend Derek, an auto mechanic (whose body may or may not be infested with termites), who loses his cool carrying her up the stairs to their apartment.

"[A] wry and unnerving story of bad love gone rotten. [Mohr] has a generous understanding of his characters, whom he describes with an intelligence and sensitivity that pulls you in. This is no small achievement."
—**NEW YORK TIMES BOOK REVIEW**
EDITORS' CHOICE

"Explodes with pyrotechnic prose. *Termite Parade* flaunts the big burning heart on Mohr's sleeve, wildly tossing it about to light the way in a relentless search for answer to the unanswerable."
—**RAIN TAXI**

"Mohr writes like John Milton living in a garbage dump, and always infuses a tiny thread of what might be hope."
—**SACRAMENTO BEE**
A BEST READ OF 2010

"Mohr's storytelling is so absorbing that *Termite Parade* does not read like an analytical rumination; if he is examining the very nature of these characters under a microscope, he at least lets the specimens speak for themselves."
—**SAN FRANCISCO CHRONICLE**

Praise for Joshua Mohr's
Some Things That Meant the World to Me

When Rhonda was a child — abandoned and ignored by his mother, abused and misguided by his mother's boyfriend — he imagined the rooms of his home drifting apart from one another like separating continents. Years later, after an embarassing episode as an adult, Rhonda's inner-child appears, leading him to a trapdoor in an unlikely place that will force him to finally confront his troubled past.

"Meet Rhonda, a man who spends his haunted, liquor-fueled days Dumpster diving for redemption. With his first line — "I'd like to brag about the night I saved a hooker's life" — debut writer Joshua Mohr sucks you into *Some Things That Meant the World to Me*. Charles Bukowski fans will dig the grit in this seedy novel, a poetic rendering of postmodern San Francisco."
—O, The Oprah Magazine
#8 of "10 Terrific Reads of 2009"

"What Joshua Mohr is doing has more in common with Kafka, Lewis Carroll, and Haruki Murakami, all great chroniclers of the fantastic. He's interested in something weirder than mere sex, drugs, and degradation."
—The Rumpus

"Where Michel Gondry would go if he went down a few too many miles of bad desert road. Replace the director's *Science of Sleep*-style clouds-of-cotton whimsy with harsh whiskey and hot sand and you get a sense for the dark world Mohr constructs."
—The Collagist

For Leota Antoinette—
Thanks for adding so much color
to my black and white world.

Copyright © 2011 by Joshua Mohr
All rights reserved.
ISBN: 978-0-9826848-9-4
Library of Congress Control Number: 2011925179

Cover photograph by Leota Antoinette Higgins.
Author photograph by Kevin Irby.

TWO DOLLAR RADIO
Books too loud to ignore

www.TwoDollarRadio.com
twodollar@TwoDollarRadio.com

"People are evil it's true,
but on the other side—
they can be gentle, too.
They decide."

The Flaming Lips

DAMASCUS

Part One

(So a guy goes into a bar... 10,000 years of bad luck...
Shambles and schnapps and Santa Claus... the artist
harpoons America... camping under man-made stars...
dead fish hanging on the walls... death threat...)

seducing the dismal

L et's start this one when a cancer patient named No Eyebrows creeps into Damascus, a Mission District dive bar.
For years the place's floor, walls, and ceiling had been
painted entirely black, but that afternoon the owner added a new
element, smashing twenty mirrors and gluing the shards to the
ceiling so the pieces shimmered like stars, transforming Damascus into a planetarium for drunkards: dejected men and women
stargazing from barstools.

When the first customer of the day walked in and witnessed
the bar's broken-mirror constellations, he said to the owner,
"There must be 10,000 years of bad luck hanging here."

"That would certainly explain a few things," Owen said, who
had a heinous birthmark underneath his nose that looked like a
Hitler moustache.

Damascus always had rock and roll on the jukebox. Right
then it was AC/DC, playing the only chord progression they
knew, howling about salacious women, which was funny because
Damascus had an almost exclusively male clientele. Old drunks
talking to themselves, trying to barter the price of a Corona with
the bartender. Surly construction workers who drank from the
minute they got off work until last call. "Off-duty" mariachis
getting more tone deaf with each tilt of tequila, wearing match-
ing black outfits spotted with silver buckles that made them look
like decorated war veterans. Insipid twenty-something Caucasian
boys, their cheeks stuffed with carbohydrates and college degrees, wowed by their own flickering wits: "Here's to honor,"
one would say, "getting on her and staying on her."

There were a few female regulars, and one who haunted the place was Shambles. She had acne scars all over her cragged cheeks, pocked like the mirror-shards glued to the bar's ceiling. Skin crimped. Her hair had been bleached too many times: tips brittle, broken, crooked. Frayed bangs that fell down to her eyebrows and pointed a million directions like tassels. Her eyes used to be blue, but they'd faded to matte gray.

Shambles was the patron saint of the hand job, getting strangers off for less than the price of a parking ticket. So far tonight she'd done only one, though there would be more fondling to finance her bar tab. The night was young and full of fisted opportunities.

No Eyebrows stood next to Shambles' stool and ordered a shot of peppermint schnapps. He liked to drink it because the taste reminded him of mouthwash, in a way that stoked his hostile nostalgia, reminded him that there had been days, real days where he used mouthwash and had a family. Days long before they found tumors stuck to his lungs like poisonous barnacles.

Owen placed the huge shot down on the bar, and as No Eyebrows reached for it with a shaking hand, Shambles looked at his sallow skin, the way it clung to him like a layer of film on cold chicken broth. Most people were shocked by his appearance because he reinforced the fact that everyone was going to die. People pursed their lips and averted their eyes, shaming him into near invisibility with the verve of their avoidances, trying not to ogle the prowling dead.

Shambles, however, wasn't deterred or deflected or weirded out by his appearance. She saw him as a business opportunity, dollar signs, an untapped masturbation market (though she wouldn't establish eye contact with him during the act itself; she never did with any of 'em).

"Do you mind if I drink with you?" Shambles said to No Eyebrows, then asked Owen to pour her another whiskey.

"I'd like that," No Eyebrows said. "Thanks."

Owen brought her drink and said, "This is your last shot." He resented how openly she flaunted her zeal to fondle the customers because the only hands that had been on him in over a year were incidental brushes. Often, he felt like a person collecting tolls at a bridge, interacting with hundreds, thousands of people every day but never knowing any of them. They approached, idled, vanished, and he was stuck in his tiny shack (Damascus, in this case), awaiting the next impatient exchange.

Shambles frowned at Owen's warning. She waved him away. He could be testy. A nice man, but definitely grumpy. Not to mention his atrocious birthmark. She tried not to stare at it every time they spoke, but she couldn't help herself: it was like he had a third nipple on his upper lip.

"Why are you thanking me for drinking with you?" she said to No Eyebrows.

"I was raised right. Cheers," he said, holding his schnapps up in the air like a Bible in a minister's hand, a prop to retrofit the fragile world.

Instead of echoing *cheers* though, Shambles crashed her glass into his, spilling whiskey on her fingers, and said, "To livers aching like shin splints."

He laughed. They drained their shots. Flushed faces from the spirits. Humidity spreading through their private ecosystems.

"I've never seen you here before," she said.

"First time."

"What brought you into this dump?"

"I was incredibly parched."

"You don't seem like you have much in common with these deadbeats."

He pointed at some of the men in their vicinity. "Doesn't that make them the lucky ones?"

Shambles didn't know how to respond to this, didn't know what to do with that kind of tactless honesty amongst strangers, especially in bars where men and women typically honed their espionage, cloaked in personas. Deception was the norm: cab drivers disclosed that they were venture capitalists; rickety alcoholics morphed into ex-athletes; those with anonymous office jobs had recently retired from the cubicle because of an important invention. (One bloke even tried to convince a woman that he masterminded the Caps Lock key.)

Every interchange was a con.

Every night, a pitiful costume party.

Except here was No Eyebrows blowing the whole cycle of charades for everyone. Here he was having the audacity to be heartfelt, and what was Shambles supposed to do with someone showing *honesty*?

So instead of answering him directly she turned her attention to tawdry commerce: "How'd you like to get off?"

•••••••

Owen should have been dumping olive juice into a dirty martini, but instead he stared at Shambles guiding No Eyebrows into the bathroom. Owen sighed, worried that it would take more than some shattered mirror-shards pasted to the ceiling to really change anything around here. Maybe the art show would do the trick. It was coming up pretty quick and was going to be unorthodox to say the least. Anti-George W. Bush. Anti-war. Dead fish dangling from the walls.

No one knew this yet, but the show was actually going to change a number of things, including lives. It would end up being covered on CNN, the BBC, all the major news outlets. Torching its way across the internet news feeds and social sites as one of the most surreal, outlandish, unbelievable stories to come around in a while. But we'll get to all that soon enough.

•••••••

As soon as they were in Damascus's bathroom he yanked his pants down. Shambles locked the door, showed him a rubber. "It's twenty bucks with this." She shook the little silver square back and forth, business savvy. "Forty without." She pulled a lube-tube from her purse and squirted it in her palm, working it around.

The bathroom light fluttered off and on, a faulty bulb, making a noise like a fly smacking into a window.

"Forty, forty," No Eyebrows said, bending at the waist and fumbling through his pockets for money. He stood up and gave her two twenties.

"My rules," she said. "Don't touch me. Don't cum on me. Or I'll scream." This was the same canned speech she spewed to everyone she brought in here.

"Of course. I'll even buy you a drink later," said No Eyebrows, hoping this offer would make him feel less seedy, but it made him feel worse, actually, its macho predictability.

"Chivalrous," she said, almost laughing. This was what passed for small talk while your hand was lodged in a man's crotch. She slid her wet fist down him, noticing he was so bald that he didn't even have pubic hair, just tiny red sores on his abdomen. "You must be from Camelot."

"Kansas City originally," he said and smiled at her, but she didn't smile back. "Does that feel good?" Shambles said.

"It feels great," closing his eyes so he didn't have to watch the droopy thing flop around. God damn chemo. Closing his eyes so nothing existed except her hand on his body. This wasn't about sex. This was survival.

"Faster?"

"Just keep touching me."

Shambles maintained her speed, looked at him more closely since he'd cinched his eyes. She didn't understand what he was doing at Damascus in the first place: he was sick, no doubt seriously sick, yet here he was in the bar's bathroom with his pants around his ankles.

Someone jiggled the locked door and knocked on it.

"Just a minute," Shambles said, increasing her speed.

No Eyebrows moaned feebly. Grinned. Remembering when

his wife used to touch his body. He'd taken it all for granted, every fingertip traipsing across his skin. The way his wife, Sally, used to run her hands through his hair when he couldn't sleep, and now there was no hair, no wife, no daughter, no chance of living more than another couple months. He'd removed himself from his family, vanishing from the North Bay into San Francisco, because what was the point of prolonging a life mired in illness? Why postpone death, if it was the only way to hush the squealing reality that he'd never see his daughter grow up? He stopped going to his appointments at the hospital. Prescriptions unfilled. Phone calls never returned. If these were his last weeks, he wouldn't waste them saving himself.

Now No Eyebrows glanced at Shambles, who averted her gaze to the ceiling's wavering light. For some reason it was harder to resist eye contact with him—something about his whole honest spiel, the way his disease was exposed while the rest of us tried to veil our glitches and bankruptcies and stale sins. Shambles found him enticing, which hadn't happened in a long time, a man seeming to be anything but a danger, a liability.

Someone knocked on the door again.

"More time," Shambles said.

"Why can't I touch you?" No Eyebrows said.

Her hand slowed down. She wanted to look at him but beat back the urge. "It's one of my rules."

"I know. But I'm wondering why."

Still resisting, her eyes fixed on the shuddering light: "Because I'm not a whore."

"How would that make you a whore if I touched your shoulder?"

"Don't touch my shoulder."

"I'm not going to."

"Do you want me to stop?" She let go of him and he shook his head. "Then don't ask any more questions."

"Please, I need you to touch me."

"No more questions." She fumbled for it, squeezed it harder. "Do you like that?" she said, and he said, "Don't stop touching me," and someone knocked on the door again and No Eyebrows threw his head back: every disappearing detail of his disappearing life dwindled while Shambles touched his body, and he felt pleasure, actual pleasure, this was the first hand on him in months that didn't belong to a doctor or nurse, and thirty seconds later he came, gasping for air and life and hope.

········

She let a few moments go by so he could gather himself, then Shambles turned around to wash her hands, using Damascus's green soap that smelled like menthol cigarettes. Finally, she let herself look him in the eyes and asked, "Why were you asking about my touching rule?"

"I don't understand it."

"I don't know you."

"I don't know you either, and I need you to touch me," No Eyebrows said.

"Why?"

He pointed at his face. "Do you know who wants to touch this monster?"

She didn't say anything, shook her head slowly. She saw his disease all over him, and she wondered what he saw in her. Probably a has-been, a hooker. She couldn't blame him. Her sicknesses were harder to inspect, caged under the skin, captives within a captive.

"No one wants to touch me," he said.

"I want to." She didn't know what else to say, what was there to say? "You're not a monster; lots of people are sick."

"This is all that's left of me," he said, still pointing at his gaunt face. "I'm withering."

"It's okay," Shambles said and pointed at her own face. "So am I." Then she sent her finger toward the wall, indicating the other deadbeats in Damascus. "We all are."

The bathroom's failing light bulb kept flashing, stuttering, buzzing.

"Can I pay to touch your shoulder?" he said.

"My shoulder?"

"Please." He stuck a hand in his pocket, pulling out some more money. He counted forty and held it out to her. "I want to feel your skin. Nothing dirty, I promise. Just your shoulder."

How could Shambles deny him such a naked want? And how could she accept any money if touching her shoulder was going to mean so much?

She shook her head, pushed his hand away, didn't answer until their eyes locked again. "I don't want your money."

"Please take it."

"No."

"Please," he begged.

"I don't want it," she said and stepped forward and took him in her arms, right there in Damascus's bathroom. She hugged him and he hugged her, and they stood: an old Tom Waits song seeped through the walls from the jukebox, the sink dripped, the toilet ran, the light flickered its paltry wattage like the gloomiest disco ball in the world.

the splendid asylum of impersonating kris kringle

There were other things happening in the world, of course, in the fall of 2003. A magnanimous worker at a corporate café agreed to donate one of her kidneys to a regular customer. An elderly blind man bowled a perfect game. There was a tornado in Brooklyn. A veteran of Operation Iraqi Freedom named Sam, a marine who'd been back in the Bay Area for nearly a month, was let out of the drunk tank, having no idea what he'd done to end up there, feeling his nose and knowing it was broken and laughing about it, happy about it—this was the sort of anarchy he'd been missing. The current American president, George W. Bush, spent the day posing for portraits with injured soldiers recuperating (physically) at a hospital in Bethesda, Maryland. In San Francisco, in the Mission District, Owen and his birthmark braved the windy streets the morning after Shambles and No Eyebrows' assignation in the bathroom, walking toward Ritualz café. As he made his way down Folsom Street, a man and his daughter, seven years old, saw Owen. She pointed at him: "Daddy, look, it's Adolf Hitler."

Her father gazed at Owen, chuckled, said to him, "Sorry about that. We watch a lot of the History Channel."

"Maybe she should watch more cartoons." This wasn't the first time somebody had made the connection between his birthmark and a Hitler moustache, but it was the first time a child had said so to Owen's face.

"Maybe," the father said, "but to her credit, the resemblance is uncanny."

The resemblance was not uncanny from Owen's prerogative: it was unfortunate. Unfair. Unequalled in its unkindness.

Unbelievably unlucky. Undermining others' understanding of his unsavory undertaking. The word *uncanny* only applied if the terrible smudge wasn't fastened to your face. If strangers didn't stare. If Revv, the only bartender you gainfully employed, whose god damn checks you signed, didn't perform surreptitious Hitler-salutes behind your back, mouthing, "*Sieg Heil!*" and laughing, all at your birthmark's expense.

"You might want to teach her some manners," Owen said.

The father didn't answer. Instead, he noticed his daughter's shoe was untied and leaned down to fix the knot.

"Maybe it's just me," Owen kept going, "but it's pretty rude to call someone a dictator who incinerated six million Jews."

It's hard to say why this one interaction affected Owen so explicitly; impossible to pinpoint why this conversation prodded Owen's anger out of its dormancy. Was it a simple accumulation: had there been so many birthmark cracks over the years that this was the proverbial straw that dropped the camel to its knees, unable to stand again and continue its aimless mope? Was it his hangover that morning? Was it that his hangover that morning was the same one he'd had every day for the past forty years? Did it feel more violating because of the girl's young age? Was it the mirrors he'd broken, their bad luck? Was it that he'd again betrayed the promise he'd made last night not to drink during his shift behind the bar? Was it that not drinking one night behind the bar actually felt like an accomplishment? Was it that he felt friendless? Was it that Wednesday the only two places he went were his apartment and Damascus? Was it that those two places were often his only stops in a twenty-four hour period? Was it that sometimes if he felt too drunk to stagger home, he hoisted a sleeping bag on one of the bar's pool tables and spent the night there? Was it waking up the next morning, cocooned, disoriented, thirsty, then as he realized where he was, the onslaught of guilt and shame and helplessness? Was it the names he called himself within the walls of his skull: *loser rotten stinking alcoholic waste of air*? Was it the blood in his stool? Why didn't he go to rehab? AA? Sell the bar? Was it the streets that particular morning, more grimy, the homeless scattered on the sidewalks, refugees from their own addictions and pasts, feces streaked on buildings, broken bottles everywhere, maimed pigeons coercing, graffiti scribbled on storefronts? Was it his sexual irrelevance? Was it that the 49ers were in the middle of a losing season or was it that during his time off from Damascus his phone only rang if it was his niece, Daphne, checking up on him or Revv calling in sick? Was it that he had no other "friends" except the ones that schmoozed for free cocktails? Was it that his bar was barely breaking even, that there had been neither progress nor faltering in Damascus's fiscal intake, that it had been almost exactly the same the entire eighteen years he'd owned it? Why did life lurch on smeared in the same coagulated details?

The young girl's father said to her, while holding her shoelace, "See how I made these two bunny ears, pudding? The last step is to tie the bunny ears in a knot."

"I'm not Hitler," Owen said.

"Tie the ears?" the girl asked her father.

"Precisely," he said, grinning that dopey parental grin, genetic amazement.

"Let me get this straight," Owen said, "she knows who Hitler is but can't tie her own shoes?" He wiped his face. He was sweating that thick, marbled hangover sweat. The kind that shoved its way through the skin like coffee pooling and pushing past a filter—heavy and hot and aromatic.

"Don't listen to the man, pudding. He must be having a tough morning." The father finished tying her shoe, then looked at Owen. "Actually, it's pretty amazing that a child her age is informed enough to spot a facial similarity between a total stranger and one of the most recognizable figures in history."

"Congratulations, you're doing a great job as a parent," Owen said. "Usually, a woman has to get into her thirties or forties to make me feel like complete shit, but your daughter has already got it figured out."

"Hey, hey," the father said to Owen. "Watch your mouth."

"Now you're worried about *my* manners," Owen said. "Good luck to you and your troll." Not catching what he'd done until the words were out of his mouth. Not realizing that he'd just insulted a child until it was too late.

Then the man rushed at him, and Owen couldn't believe the speed with which the father's temper had savagely blossomed. Maybe that was what it was like to be a parent—a love so fertile and harsh that you did anything to protect your young.

"Please," Owen said, but the father's bull-rush didn't slow and he shoved Owen hard in the solar plexus, knocking the wind out of him.

"You ever talk about my kid like that again, I'll break your nose."

Owen staggering backward, struggling for air, attempting to gather himself to grovel: "Please, I don't want any trouble. I'm sorry. I shouldn't have said it. Please."

"It's pathetic to talk to a child like that," the father said. "Do you know that you're a pathetic human being?" The father walked back to his daughter and said, "I'm sorry you had to see that, pudding."

"What happened, Daddy?"

"He's a mean man who said something he shouldn't have."

"He's a mean man," the girl echoed.

"Yes, he is," the father said.

Owen watched them walk away. He almost started crying. He swore off booze. Again. He promised himself not a drop during his shift that night, not one drop. Again. He cut up 21st Street toward Ritualz, hating himself for what he'd just done and hating that the little girl was right: he was a mean man. He was Hitler. No matter what he did, Owen was doomed to reel through the rest of his days, reminding everyone of the Holocaust.

Owen walked by a homeless man who'd scattered on the sidewalk the items he'd found, swapped, or stolen. These were laid out on a blanket to entice pedestrians. There were some clothes, a single CD, a naked Barbie doll, a broken sewing machine, a bunch of old cassettes, mostly Motown, and a cracked black case for an acoustic guitar. The guy also had six issues of *The New Yorker* from the early nineties with tattered, water-damaged pages, stiff and toothed at the edges. Nothing highfalutin or of any real monetary value, but as Owen walked toward the end of the man's paltry sale, he saw something worthy of another style of appraisal.

He saw the Santa suit.

He saw asylum.

Owen stopped in front of the costume. He imagined all those part-time workers portraying Santa at malls around the country come December. Their true identities hidden under a façade of happy associations. He needed to bury the Hitler costume he couldn't take off under the image of this Yuletide superhero.

The homeless guy held a harmonica in his hand, though he hadn't played a note since Owen had been in earshot.

"How much for the Santa suit?" Owen asked.

The wind picked up a bit, fog drifting from the Castro and through the Mission. A car was being hooked to a tow truck across the street. Someone was taping Xeroxed copies of a missing cat poster over an abandoned storefront; information leading to Chip Whiskers' safe return would result in a handsome reward.

"Twenty bucks."

"But it's filthy."

"Then don't buy it. Someone else will. Christmas is coming." He put the harmonica in his mouth and played a series of carefree notes to illustrate his ambivalence about the transaction.

Owen sighed, saddened that he'd been bested by a homeless merchant. "Twenty it is."

"Wear that uniform well. Make Kris Kringle proud."

Owen removed his coat and began to put the suit on over his clothes. The Santa pants were a little short for him, revealing an inch of his jeans, a little tight in the waist. The coat, too, was snug, sleeves only coming three quarters of the way down his forearms. But he didn't care. Once he slipped the beard and hat on, every man, woman, and child would see Santa Claus and think to themselves *yes, yes, yes, now there's a friendly face.*

· · · · · · · ·

A college student stood out front of Ritualz in a Che Guevara T-shirt, holding a clipboard. He asked Owen, "Does Santa want to sign a petition to legalize marijuana?"

"I stay out of politics."

"Who said anything about politics, bro; this is about our god-given right to smoke the sticky-icky."

Owen only shrugged and went inside the café, ordered a double espresso. The young hipster behind the counter sported full sleeves of tattoos, inch-long crows flying up her arms; she said to him, "Can I give you my Christmas list?"

"Of course."

"All I want is for my boyfriend to go to rehab."

"I'll see what I can do."

"And the new PJ Harvey CD."

"Noted."

"But if I had to choose one or the other, definitely Seth getting into rehab. I can't remember the last time I saw him sober. Last night I caught him licking a stick of butter as a midnight snack. This morning he was drinking rum in the shower when I left."

"I will do my best to help him." The crows on the backs of her wrists had their beaks open, shrieking. Owen tried to hand her three dollars but she shook it away. Then she looked around, and once convinced that her perimeter was safe from any managerial condemnation, she whispered to Santa, "Your money is no good around here," which was the first time that had ever been the case, before his transformation from villain to saint.

········

Elation thumped through Owen as he walked out of the café. Energetic and motivated to cruise the neighborhood and watch people's reactions to his new protective skin.

The public proved very interested in chatting with him. There were "Ho, ho, hos," and "Hey, Santa, what are you doing out in October, consumer research?" and "Don't forget about me, I've been nice all year, except to my brother, but he's a total a-hole," and even an, "I just got laid off by my start-up. Are you guys hiring at the North Pole?"

All of these were met with the warmest wishes and largest smiles from Mr. Claus, as Owen gushed enthusiasm in his new starring role. No one was ordering a whiskey sour and defiantly staring at his birthmark. No one threw up in the bathroom and told Owen he better go "swab the decks." Revv wasn't lobbing the secret "*Sieg Heil!*" when he thought you couldn't see the crude charade (and sometimes lobbing it when he damn well knew you could see him, but that was the sort of smart ass the kid was).

Point is that these were no small victories for Owen. Overdue. You might wonder why he didn't grow a beard and cover the damn thing up, but it wasn't that easy, his hair follicles unable to penetrate the abomination's cruel girth. Way back when, he'd even pondered plastic surgery, but his insurance snickered at the idea elective procedures might fall under their jurisdiction.

Sure, the fog and wind were chilly, but Owen didn't care, didn't notice them, as he paraded like a holiday peacock.

"I'm never taking this damn suit off. Ever," he said to himself, preparing to perform a belly-laugh for a group of people coming his way. One of them was already calling out from down the block, "We love you, Santa; what kind of cookies should we leave out this year?"

bile and lies

That night, Shambles was back at the bar wearing her *I'd rather be divorced than in denial* T-shirt, which would have been quite a conversation piece had it not been for the reaction Owen's Santa suit impelled in the clientele, nearly all the men and women of Damascus instantaneously regressing into children as they laid eyes on him. Even for those who did not come of age celebrating Christmas, Saint Nick's presence was an antidote, however temporary, for apathy.

The normal blotch of angst that the bar wore like too much rouge was suddenly blended with a deft and savvy hand. The mood among the disillusioned more jovial. Charisma flashed and stuttered in a few sets of eyes, like static on malfunctioning televisions. The same ol' drinks tasted divine. The songs playing on the jukebox—the tired old rock and roll songs that spun every night—didn't sound angry or plaintive.

Hell, we can go ahead and just say it: people actually seemed happy.

People. Happy. In Damascus.

Three of the ecstatic patrons were Shambles and her two favorite drinking buddies, Maya and Karla. They all had empty shot glasses in front of them and were engaged in the sport of "man-slaughter," as they liked to call it: hour after hour discussing and dissecting and battering their ex-husbands and ex-boyfriends and ex-lovers and every stranger they'd ever picked up. The women were pretty drunk. Karla spoke next in their rotation: "Just once I want to have sex with a guy whose cock is so big he has to claim it as a dependent on his taxes."

"Gross," Maya said. "I'll settle for one who can keep it hard for more than fifteen minutes."

Karla kept going: "Or so big he can ride it down a snowy knoll like it's a toboggan."

"I'll settle for one who doesn't make me feel bad about myself," Shambles said and brushed her bleached bangs to the side. Hanging into her eyes, dry and unruly like tinsel, they needed to be trimmed.

"Or has to buy it a seat next to him on an airplane and fasten its seat belt and get it a Jack and Coke from the stewardess..."

"I hate it when men try to be charming," Maya said. "Nothing weirder than getting a guy out of the bar and he turns into a philosopher."

"That's why I keep them in Damascus's bathroom," Shambles said. "No time to recite Shakespeare while my hand's in their business."

Karla snapped into the flow of the conversation: "I once took a guy home and while he came he shouted '*It was a dark and stormy night!*'"

"What did you do?"

"What could I do? He's a meteorologist." Karla ordered another round of whiskeys from Owen, who refilled their glasses and said, "These are on me, oh tempting sirens."

"Very generous, Santa," Maya said.

"Too generous," Shambles said. "What's in it for you? Are you some kind of pervert?"

"Not every deed requires a motive," he said and strutted down the bar, shouting back at them, "but yes, I'm known for my perversions all around the North Pole. Never leave me alone with a reindeer." Not that anyone could see it buried behind his fake beard, but he was smiling.

The women drank their complimentary shots. Then someone tapped Shambles' shoulder. It was No Eyebrows. "What brings you back to this dump?" she said.

"Can I buy you ladies a drink?" No Eyebrows said and motioned to Owen.

Maya and Karla only peered at No Eyebrows for a few seconds before whispering secrets about how strange he looked—bald of even a single hair, skin falling forward like an avalanche, face gray like toxic oatmeal.

"Another round for the girls here," No Eyebrows said, surprised by the Santa costume, not as tickled by it as everyone else. It reminded him not of his own childhood, but of the daughter he'd recently abandoned. Before his diagnosis, he and his wife, Sally, used to stay up on Christmas Eve wrapping presents at the last possible minute, drinking red wine and cracking up. She couldn't believe how bad his gifts looked, paper crinkled and bunched, one present not even totally covered, a whole edge of the package visible. "They never drilled this into us in law school," he'd say. Sally always had to fix the ones he'd done, and he'd sit on the floor next to her, pretending to pay attention, promising to do better next year. What a luxury, next year.

"I'll have one, too," No Eyebrows said to Owen.

"No schnapps for you tonight?" Owen asked.

"I'll enjoy whatever elixir these ladies are having."

Owen poured the shots. Shambles held hers up in the air and repeated her cocktail mantra: "To livers aching like shin splints."

Everyone drank; No Eyebrows made the bile-rollicking-in-the-esophagus face, mouth watering in an awful way. "Can I talk to you in the bathroom?" he said to Shambles, and her friends cackled.

•••••••

"Julia Roberts in *Pretty Woman*," Shambles said to him. "The hooker with a heart of gold." She washed her hands after it was over, after No Eyebrows was all over the floor in harsh streaks. "That's who you're looking for, but that's not me. Pull your pants up."

"I'm not here to save you," he said and followed her orders—zip, snap, fastening of belt. "I just want to get to know you."

"I'm not even a hooker," Shambles said. "I just do jerk-offs. If you're looking for hookers talk to my friend Karla out there."

"Let me take you on a date."

Here, Shambles disregarded her experience, that voice of vast hand job knowledge that told her to walk out of here and not see him anymore. The crass edification she'd accumulated over the last eighteen months, night after night of strange dicks, bringing unknown men to orgasm. "I don't date clients." Shambles laughed awkwardly, dried her hands on her pants because there weren't any paper towels left in the bathroom.

"Just dinner. Do you eat dinner?"

"I'm more of a grazer."

"Sashimi. Easy to digest."

"I don't like raw things."

"Some of it's cooked. Barbecued eel."

"Why?"

"Why eel?"

"Why would you want to get to know me?" she said.

"I stumbled into this bar for a reason."

"You were thirsty."

"That's not it."

"It was raining."

"No, it wasn't."

"Accept this fact," Shambles said. Her hands still a bit damp, she ran them again down her pants. "This is all I can give you."

········

But he did not accept her assertion, and there was a stretch of consecutive nights, nine straight to be exact, of No Eyebrows coming into Damascus to see her. Their ritual was always the same: he offered to buy her a drink; she accepted; they went into the bathroom; she jacked him off; he asked her on dates repeatedly; she refused; he asked, "Why, why, I don't understand, is it the way I look?" and she always told him it had nothing to do with him, that it was just a rule she had, not to get involved with anyone from the office, which was what she called the bathroom at Damascus—the office. No Eyebrows wanted to push the argument, always dropping the issue right on the brink of her telling him this whole arrangement was over. But something in his persistency degraded her defenses. She didn't understand his motivations, started thinking about him, wondering if maybe she should make an exception to her rule about office romances. Why not? Shambles had quite a consecutive night streak at Damascus herself, months on end, and maybe she was due for a night on the town.

She told Maya what she was debating while they sat on their normal stools, playing the recycled agony of rock and roll ballads on the jukebox. (The sadness had crept back into the music as people built up tolerances to seeing Owen's Santa suit on a daily basis, much like the required levels of liquor upped over time to achieve optimum inebriation.)

"I'd let him take me to dinner," Maya said.

"He likes strangers to jerk him off."

"He likes you to jerk him off. Since when are you the fetish police?"

A song came on from Shambles' past, one of her ex-husband's favorites, a whiny British melody. She tried not to think about that sham-marriage, its fragile existence, but every time someone played this song, she saw all the ways it had seeped its sustenance—love and excitement and trust and possibilities—until there was nothing left except boredom, resentment. Nothing left to do but admit defeat and abandon each other. She had once asked her husband as their marriage was curdling, "Do you remember when we used to have sex?" and he said, "Of course. That's why we don't do it anymore."

"Don't joke."

"Who's joking?"

Now there was a man begging Shambles to touch him. A man who needed her hands on him. She said to Maya, "You're right. I'll tell him tonight. When's the last time someone wanted to get to know this old hag?"

• • • • • • • •

The problem was that No Eyebrows didn't show up that night. Shambles sat at the bar, refusing all her regular customers, even turning away some greenhorns because she wanted to tell him *YES*. She wanted to go out to a restaurant with a man. A man who seemed respectable. Sure, she met him in the office— toilet instead of a desk—but he was always polite, pleasant, and most importantly, he seemed interested in her, even if she didn't know why.

She nursed her whiskey, not wanting to get too wasted. Pacing herself wasn't one of Shambles' fortes. Maya and Karla tried their best to slow her down, though neither could claim pacing to be a strength of theirs either. As it got late, her drinking picked up and soon she shot whiskey faster than usual, mad at herself, humiliated. She stayed at the bar twenty minutes after Owen said he wanted to go home, and as he took the empties outside for the homeless to collect, Shambles lurched out alone, sullen, wondering why she'd subjected herself to hope.

• • • • • • • •

The next night Shambles went back to the office. Unconsciously, she still waited for him, but a girl had to earn a living, had to pay for tuna sandwiches and chicken potpies somehow.

Shambles took a Santa Barbara-looking young man—Hawaiian shirt, flip-flops, holes in the knees of his jeans—into her office, telling him the rules, *don't touch me or cum on me*, the price with and without a rubber.

He smiled and said, "Bareback, baby."

She put the rubber away and squirted lube in her palm. He dropped his pants. Even his dick was tan.

"For an extra twenty, will you do it topless?" he said, rubbing himself hard. "I love seeing tits."

"I don't think so."

"But tits are cool."

"Sorry."

"Come on, I need to see some cool tits!"

"No."

"An even hundred?" he offered, and Shambles tried to shimmy out of her top without getting lube on the sleeve.

·······

After Santa Barbara vacated the bathroom, Shambles washed her hands. No matter how hard she scrubbed, she couldn't get the scent of him off of her, semen like garlic oil.

She sat on the closed toilet, leaned her head against the wall, had the urge to cry. Maya knocked on her office door and said, "Are you okay?"

Shambles let her in, and they lit cigarettes. "That made me feel awful."

"Why?"

"Where is he?"

"Stop doing it to strangers until you find out about the two of you."

"Am I being stupid?"

"No. Maybe. How should I know?" Maya said.

·······

For the next two nights, Shambles planted herself at the bar with her friends, waiting. She drank whiskey and tried not to take each passing minute as a vendetta.

"He'll be here," Karla said.

"When?" Shambles chewed her nails and spit them on the floor like they were the shells of sunflower seeds.

·······

When people asked her why she and her ex split up, Shambles liked to say, "It fizzled."

This answer always confused them, waiting for an elaboration, stories of violence or infidelity or addiction. "Fizzled?"

"Petered out."

"But what finally ended it?" they wondered.

Her ex didn't get it either, didn't understand why you'd abandon a relationship that didn't have an obvious problem. Exciting? No. But stable. And he couldn't believe she wanted the unknown instead of a stable, albeit humdrum, life.

She never gave him a very good answer, and she hadn't found one since, so she always ending up lying to her snooping audience: "He gambled. A lot. Lost all our money."

"That's a tough vice," they'd say, now satisfied.

....

By the next weekend—ten days since No Eyebrows' last appearance—Shambles assumed he would never come back, felt tricked by him, duped, another dumb woman believing another man's lies. So instead of turning some of the jerk-off candidates away like she'd been doing, she took all contestants tonight. It was only ten o'clock and she'd done four already.

It poured rain outside; San Francisco had already had five inches that day, more than its sewers were capable of processing. Water collected in the streets and sidewalks. The power was out in the lower Haight and Castro Districts.

No Eyebrows was soaked when he came into Damascus and walked over to Shambles.

"I'm not working tonight," she said to him, a little drunk.

"Why?" He wiped some water from his face, then his wet hands on his pants.

"Carpal tunnel," she said and shook her wrist sarcastically.

"Can I buy you a drink?" He asked Revv—it was Owen's night off—to get Shambles another one, and ordered himself a beer. "Have you thought about dinner?"

"No," she said. "I mean, yes I've thought about it, and no, I won't have it with you." Shambles couldn't understand him: it had been well over a week: what planet did this guy live on?

The drinks came; they both stared at theirs; he emptied most of his beer in two sips. "I'm sorry for asking again," he said. "I should have known better."

Shambles put her drink to her mouth, using the booze as a roadblock so she didn't say any placating words.

He finished his final sip of foam. "Well, this is good-bye." He turned to leave.

"Where have you been?"

"What do you mean?"

"I thought you'd be back sooner."

"From what?"

"I mean, be back sooner to see me."

"I have cancer. It's been a rough stretch."

It hadn't even occurred to Shambles that his absence might have had nothing to do with her. And that made her feel self-important. And that made her sad. "Why didn't you just tell me that?"

"I come here to forget," he said and took a couple steps toward the door. "Sorry to have bothered you."

"Don't go."

"Why?"

"Would you like one for the road?" she said and three minutes later greased up her palm and grabbed him hard. "This is the last one," she said, starting to slide. "I don't want to see you again." And at that moment, she meant it. She couldn't imagine seeing him another time, couldn't imagine waiting to see him. She stayed in Damascus, in its grimy bathroom, because she didn't wanna be out amidst the pelting malaise, and she was okay with the straitjacket she'd put on herself, the feelings in her heart she'd turned off like old fuses. Okay making men cum to earn a living because she didn't find it any more degrading than dealing with her ex-husband, her ex-jobs, waiting tables or answering phones in a real estate office or cleaning rooms in an assisted living facility, or any other ex-details from those ex-lives, when she was other women altogether. This version of herself had been totally her idea, not influenced by her parents or her ex or the fettering obliviousness of youth: this Shambles was self-made and she was proud of that. Sure, there were days she didn't like this remix any better than the others. Sure, some men made her feel cheap, but wouldn't that have been true outside her office?

In the Hollywood story of Shambles' life, she didn't want to be saved unless it was genuine salvation. Nothing tritely choreographed. No cheap resurrection. No philosophical moonshine. If she was going to be saved it had to be undiluted. Easy answers or false projections would be worse than dying. Her movie couldn't end with sentimental schlock or phony closure. She'd rather be left tethered to the stake about to be eaten by the mythical dragon than have a prince racing on a white horse to unbind her wrists. She was fine with the bank robbers executing her to show the crack team of police negotiators that they were ruthless professionals. Okay with freezing to death on a flotsam piece of wood in the Atlantic, after the *Titanic* finished its dramatic breech.

But then it dawned on Shambles that No Eyebrows might be the perfect hero for her Hollywood movie: he was dying. He couldn't save her forever, just a little while. A makeshift sanctuary. A doomed one.

The pace of her hand quickened. No Eyebrows moaned and threw his head back. He reached out and touched her shoulder.

"Don't," she said and shook off his hand. "Don't touch me." Shambles jacked him off faster, unrelenting, squeezing him as tight as she could.

Again his hand moved around to her back, up and down her spine.

"Stop touching me."

"You make me feel like there's more than tumors and toxins," he mumbled.

And Shambles didn't tell him to stop again, didn't step back, or take her hand off of him. She stood there and let his clumsy hands fumble her back, her spine, rubbing its bumpiness.

"I've got tumors all over my back," he said. "They hide in between my vertebrae. But your back feels perfect. It gives me hope."

Shambles took her free hand and ran it behind his balls, lightly scratching the skin.

"My last PET scan showed nine new tumors on my back. Nine! They ache. It's like a rotisserie spinning. I can feel each cell divide. I used to name them, but now there's too many."

"What did you name them?"

"I named the first one Erica after my daughter."

She collapsed into his crotch, and in this action she not only lapped his pathos and regrets, but her own. She tasted their personal ruins.

"No more chemo," he said.

Shambles couldn't look up at him, couldn't believe she was doing this in the first place, ran her tongue along its underside, tracing the vein, using her hand for friction.

"No more metastases... no portacath... no gamma-knife surgery..." he said. His body shook, first in his thighs, then jolts through his torso. He made choking noises and slammed his hands against his hips. "It's not fucking fair!"

Shambles took every drop of it in and collapsed to the floor and he fell backward onto the toilet seat, laboring to breathe, sweat running down his face, the faintest smile wobbling there. She ran her hand across her mouth, the taste in it acrid, a rotting lemon. She watched the huge breaths go in and out of his body. Something sort of innocent about him. How long had it been since she'd even thought of innocence? How long since she'd seen something in the world besides blasphemy, something that wasn't smeared in bile and lies?

one mysterious piece

Acouple days before No Eyebrows and Shambles reunited in her office, a guy leaned out his car window a bit past three a.m. and said to Owen, "Will you blow into my steering wheel, Santa Claus?"

It startled Owen, as he hadn't seen the man sitting in the car and also because his niece, Daphne, was walking out of Damascus with him. He bulged with overprotection, much like the father had done when he thought Owen threatened his daughter, despite the fact that Daphne was a grown woman. He might not have been any kind of badass or black-belt, but Daph was the only family Owen had, and he'd have done anything for her.

The streets were pretty quiet, except for the occasional cluster of "friends" heading back to somebody's living room for a few grams of cocaine, filibusters about busted childhoods. Empty cabs trolled for liquored-up fares, who'd hopefully pass out in the backseats so the drivers could jack the meter by weaving around the city before shaking them awake in front of their apartments. No wind, no fog; there might have actually been a star or four faint in the sky.

"What the hell do you want from me?" Owen asked the guy, who was still leaning out his car window.

"Blow into my wheel..." he slurred, barely keeping his eyes open; Owen's anger withered when he saw the man's soggy condition. Too cooked to breathe. Sometimes seeing people in this state made Owen think that tending bar was the meanest job you could have, worse than working for the IRS because you weren't draining people's bank accounts—something that had the potential to regenerate—no, you were siphoning their pride. The guy continued: "Your reputation and generosity proceed you, Santa... my car won't start unless it whiffs sober breath... they installed this blowing thingie in my wheel so I couldn't drive drunk no more... but we can show them."

"I don't think I can help you," Owen said.

"Why is everyone always saying that?"

"Take a taxi. Don't get another DUI, pal."

"That's why god invented chewing gum, and I've got a spankin' new pack."

"I don't think it was god who invented gum."

"The real Santa Claus would help. What about you, lady?" the guy asked Daph. "Wanna make a quick twenty bucks? Easy money: just one blow in my wheel."

"Blow in your wheel? As a proud lesbian, I take offense at your offer," she said, looking at her uncle, the two of them laughing a bit. Daph knew she wasn't supposed to think this was funny, but what could she do? Sometimes you crossed paths with someone so down on their luck, someone so far behind the eight ball that they couldn't even see the eight ball anymore. It was a memory, miles away.

"Thanks for nothing, Santa!" the guy barked. "Who left you those homemade fig bars in Patterson, New Jersey, back in the '80s, huh, Santa? Who stayed up past his bedtime baking so your blood sugar didn't crash while delivering all those presents? Byron Settles did, you selfish prick. Byron Settles cared and this is the thanks I get? Oh, wow, man, you make me wish I was a Jew or a Muslim."

"I'll pay for your cab," Owen said. "Otherwise, you'll need bail money for Christmas. Here." He pulled fifty bucks from his pocket and held it out to Byron.

"I can't leave my wheels here."

"I don't see any other options."

"Just let me be," Byron said, rolling his window up slowly, making a big show of it. "Let me rot. Go on your merry way. If the world is so fucked that Santa Claus won't help you out, I guess the apocalypse is coming any day now. This is Byron Settles, signing off, another goner in a world of goners, so long, good night..."

Owning a bar for so many years, Owen had spent plenty of time around serial drunk drivers. He knew that Byron would keep asking the few stragglers still out this late until some imbecile agreed to do it. Someone would think it was funny, a hilarious story to recount to friends: the time some helpless flunky bribed them with twenty bucks to blow into his steering wheel and went on his way, primed for vehicular manslaughter. It made Owen sort of mad, actually, the idea of people preying on this man's vice. He wouldn't abandon Byron Settles to the cruelty of strangers.

Owen knocked on the car's closed window. Byron cracked it a bit. "Go away, I'm having a private moment in here that's of no concern to you or anyone else that won't help me blow into my wheel. You're a disgrace to that uniform, sir. And I know about uniforms."

"You wanna duck inside for a bit?" Owen said.

"I need to get home. She's going to kill me if I stay out all night again."

"We can call and let her know you're safe. I own that bar right there."

"A bar?" Byron said, swelling with awareness, flicking his eyebrows. "Well, well, well..."

"Owen, this isn't a good idea," Daph said.

"Go on home, good-looking," Owen said to her and kissed his niece. "Byron and me are going to have a couple cups of coffee."

"Do you mind if I stick around?" she asked, though that was the last thing she wanted to do. But if Owen was nice enough to try and help this guy, the least she could do was show some solidarity, tough down a cup of coffee, not make him suffer through it alone. Daph would never do something like this without Owen instigating it. She'd have walked right past Byron on the street and had some snide names to call him in her head. Sounded coldblooded but certain battles were worth your effort and others weren't: Daph loved working with kids and would tutor a dyslexic child twenty hours straight if it meant helping her/ him learn to read. But Byron wasn't the kind of emergency that aroused Daph's compassion.

"Byron and I would love to have your company," Owen said to her.

"Ditto. I totally agree with all that," said Byron, still speaking through the cracked window. Then panic crossed his face, his one-track mind jumping away from Daphne and now fixating on the fact that his wife was going to divorce his ass if he didn't get home ASAP. "She said it point blank. You go out drinking in Sacramento; you come back to your house in Sacramento. Period. Her terms didn't seem negotiable."

"You're a long way from home," Owen said.

"Where am I?"

"San Francisco."

"Are you sure?"

"Yeah, I'm sure."

"Really really sure?"

"Yup."

"Jesus, I'm deader than I originally thought. How the hell did I get here?"

"Let's call her so she knows you're okay," Owen said.

Byron got out of the car. "You got a pool table in that joint? They say I can't drive drunk, but I can shoot pool liquored like a god damn shark."

"I have two tables," Owen said, "so long as you don't hustle me."

"I was wrong. You ain't a selfish prick. I'm glad I made you those fig bars."

The front of Owen's Santa suit was a little wet. A keg had blown earlier and suds sprayed all over him. No doubt it was in need of a laundering—one that wasn't coming any time soon.

"You can crash here," Owen said. "Sometimes I throw a sleeping bag on a pool table. You and I can both stay the night."

Byron seemed pleased with this. "That's a grade A, rock-solid plan. Thanks."

Daphne, however, was far from pleased, hearing that her uncle slept at the bar. It occurred to her that Owen might be one of those people who needed help, trailing way behind the eight ball. Her mom, god rest her soul, had eighteen months sober before dying of liver failure, and she would've given Owen some tough love, would've reminded him that there was a great big world going on outside the bar's black walls and he needed to go do some living. She needed to be a better niece. Maybe they should stop spending so much time together at Damascus, often bellying up on Owen's nights off, unless Daph had a date. They both liked movies—why didn't they ever go?

Now Owen opened up the bar's front door, turned on the lights. The three of them walked inside, and Byron Settles immediately looked up at the ceiling, wide-eyed, thrilled. See, the reason Owen and Daphne had stuck around the bar until three a.m. was that they had made clouds for the bar's starred ceiling, gluing cotton balls to old beer boxes and suspending them from fishing line. But if the mirror-shards mimicked the stars successfully (they refracted Damascus's dim light quite well), these clouds were more precarious imposters, looking like decapitated sheep.

The stars, the clouds, these wild ideas came to Owen once he'd agreed to host the art show. When it had first been pitched to him, it was a late-night scene much like this one— way after last call, Owen counting the money, vulnerable with drunkenness. He, Daph, and, Syl all had a shot of whiskey. (He'd had seven already.)

That night, Owen tried to listen as Daph's words ran at him, over him, trampled him like a startled herd of cattle. He tried, kinda, but he sort of wasn't able to at the same time. Whiskey. His head thrummed with the stuff; he felt as if a helicopter hovered a few feet over his head so he couldn't really hear her clearly and he focused most of his attention on standing up straight, and Jesus, she'd been ranting awhile. He nodded as his niece spoke. She was saying something about making the art opening more of a mixed-medium expression, more than just the paintings themselves, transcending the idea that visual art is something solely for the eyes. They'd make it an experience that encompassed other sensory detectives, most notably the nose.

"Smell," Daphne said. "Have you ever been to an art show that vanquished your sense of smell?"

"I've never been to an art show period," he said, wobbling.

And she was off again. There was something euphoric and religious in her momentum. A medium, a con artist. Words sprinting from the starting gate. Elaborate, nimble, long, sprawling sentences that Owen didn't like and didn't have the energy to follow and he wasn't too keen on arty babble anyhow, and Daph was saying something about how people had to be uncomfortable, had to be shoved from their complacencies: soldiers were dying on their behalves, and Syl's show could shake the safety of the American Petri dish. Syl planned on showcasing dead fish on the canvasses to augment her portraits of American soldiers who had died in Iraq. The dead fish would hang with the paintings and make the bar smell like a coffin. The stink attacking everyone. Reminding them of the soldiers' sacrifices.

"Do you like Syl's idea?" Daph asked him.

Owen started laughing. "You wanna hang dead fish in my bar?" Hysterical for some reason. "That will not smell good."

"No, but people will flock to see Syl's work. There's already a buzz building about it. Please?"

Whiskey wasn't his worst enemy, but it was a bigger one than Owen realized. Plus, even Dalai-Lama-sober he couldn't say no to Daph when she begged. "We better shake on it before I come to my senses," he said. The women were not about to let this opportunity wiggle away, heeding his advice, the three of them shaking on it before Owen could come anywhere near his senses.

Back to Byron as he stared straight up at Damascus's ceiling, mesmerized. "Is that... the sky?"

"My uncle is making some overdue improvements around here," Daphne said, so proud of Owen.

"I'm not just saying this," Byron said, "because you're saving my ass. Your sky is one of the most beautiful things I've ever seen."

"Thanks," Owen said, "I'll brew that pot of coffee. Truthfully, your car wouldn't have started if I blew into your wheel."

Daphne and Byron took seats at the bar; Owen went behind it, fussed with the ancient coffeemaker.

"Come on, coffee?" Byron said. "A bar after hours is like the Garden of Eden."

"Coffee was the deal," Daphne said, ready to bust balls if these two tried to get into the spirits. "Right, Owen? Coffee? *Just* coffee?!"

"Sorry, but she's the boss, Byron."

"I respect that," Byron said.

"Should we call your wife now? Get that out of the way?" Owen asked.

"What the hell am I going to say to her?"

"Tell her the truth."

Byron Settles did not look impressed with the suggestion of honesty. "No, maybe I got a couple flat tires or my car's stolen or I was abducted by space aliens."

"Level with her," Daph said. Relationship advice was one thing she loved hopping in the middle of even with a guy she'd just met. Lots of experience in domestic issues seeing as how she was always inviting girlfriends to move in after a handful of good—sometimes only average—dates. "She probably already knows."

"You're right," Byron said, "but then again, aliens might do the trick, too."

"What's your number?" Owen said, picking up the phone and dialing once Byron gave in. She answered right away. "Hi, my name's Owen and I'm a friend of Byron's... yeah... he's safe... we're just drinking some coffee and chatting... he's going to stay with me tonight... down in San Francisco." Owen held the phone out for Byron. "She'd like a word with you."

"Does she sound mad?" Byron whispered. Owen only answered by shaking the phone. Byron pursed his lips, listened as his wife read him something of a tepid riot act, then said to her, "Baby, I'm so sorry. I'll go back and see if it works better this time."

"We should give them some privacy," Daph said to Owen. They moved into the center of Damascus, under the stars and clouds, and she said, "You're a good man."

"We all get down on our luck sooner or later."

Daph pointed up at the new clouds. "Did they turn out like you hoped?"

"Not really, but they're already up there. I'm too old and lazy to fix 'em."

"What's wrong with them?" Daphne said.

"I hoped they'd give this place a bit more life but I don't know. Maybe I'm not sure what more life looks like."

Right then they both heard Byron Settles say to his wife, "Civilian life... it's got me all confused..."

"Was he in the army or something?" said Daph.

"Sounds like he might still be."

"Are you excited about the art show?"

"No. But you are. And that makes me happy. Syl seems like a good girl."

"How often do you crash on the pool table?" She was trying not to sound accusatory, but it wasn't working.

Owen shrugged. "Only when walking home is out of the question."

Then Byron Settles interrupted them with, "I'm all done. She's mad but not crazy-mad. It could have gone a lot worse."

"Glad to hear it," Owen said

"She wants me to steer clear of her for a week or so."

Owen moved back behind the bar to pour them coffees. "You're more than welcome to crash here in the meantime."

"Really?" asked Byron, and Daph thought the same thing. Owen's offer didn't surprise her, though she wished he hadn't made it, hadn't taken in this lost dog. They didn't know the first thing about Byron. He seemed harmless, but you never knew what somebody else was capable of.

"Why not?" Owen said.

"Thanks, Santa," said Byron. "Which one of you wants to shoot a game of pool? The legendary Byron of Billiardstown is ready."

True to their word, no one drank any liquor, only coffee, and they played a pool game called Cut-throat, in which three players could compete at once. Not that it was much of a match. Billiardstown must have been situated close to Sacramento because Byron could really shoot stick.

"I don't even know how I got to San Francisco," he said.

"Forget about that."

"Already did, remember?"

"You got here in one piece," Owen said. "That's all that matters."

"I know how many pieces I'm in, but what the hell is that piece made out of? That's the question that's fucking me up since I've been back."

"Iraq?"

"Sort of," Byron said.

"I'm sure there's a story there."

"Always is."

"How long have you been home?"

"Not sure right now. Ask me in the morning. And ask me again how I got here. Maybe I'll know something by then."

"Just be glad you're in one piece."

"I'm one mysterious piece of who-knows-what," Byron said and reached for his knee, that stubborn, stupid joint that locked up and twisted, left him rolling in the sand, tangled in his parachute, screaming. He tore his ACL, his MCL, ruptured his patellar tendon landing, simply landing. A paratrooper... no, a para*marine* who crippled himself placing his boots on the ground. First steps in-country were his last. One minute you were an invincible Sky Soldier of the 173rd about to grab the Bashur Airfield by its fucking nuts and flank those *hajji* cock-suckers from the north. Your unit frothing for combat. All that elite training and now it was time to knock skulls. But you hit the ground and mangled your knee. Your war was over after two seconds, two steps, and months later you were here, limping around the Bay Area, blowing off physical therapy and blowing into your steering wheel and still so ashamed, so hollow.

"Another game of Cut-throat?" Owen asked.

"You're asking for trouble," Byron said. "You're dancin' with the devil."

"Story of my life," said Owen, racking the balls.

as the artist readies herself to harpoon America

I t seemed to Syl that people let their lives close in on them. The walls creeping, your universe contracting until there wasn't room to outstretch your arms, let alone thrive. These were things she hated about adulthood—nobody used their imaginations anymore. (Do you ever grieve it, like an amputated limb, phantom twitches from this once vibrant "organ"?) Seemed like everybody had serious jobs and serious relationships and serious futures and serious children.

Syl liked to spend her mornings sitting in Dolores Park, her favorite part of the Mission District. It was basically the backyard none of the locals had, and so most days, whether socked in or sunny or wind whipping, people plopped down on the grass to enjoy a little nature. There were always dogs being walked, thrilled to be out of the studio apartments they were held captive in, their owners trading war stories with one another, maybe even flirting. Always picnics, Frisbees, children on the playground, soccer games down by the tennis courts, guerilla yoga classes, barbecues, hipsters reclining on blankets with acoustic guitars, brown-bagged beers, ironic sunglasses. Beautiful gay boys sunbathing in Speedos, even on days the sun wasn't living up to its end of the bargain. The dreadlocked entrepreneur selling pot treats from a Hefty bag slung over his shoulder like a demented Santa Claus. And don't forget the drunks, the junkies, as they curled on the grass in desperate fetal balls and dreamed of lives where vices weren't the centers of solar systems.

There were also circus performers who practiced in one of the park's upper corners, near 20th Street. These were the men and women Syl liked to watch. With a large latte in her hand she'd sit Indian-style and laugh to herself, amazed at the artistry. There might be jugglers, unicyclists, acrobats. Today they had two tightropes fastened between the palm trees for practice. One wasn't very high off the ground, maybe three feet. The other required a ladder to get to it, a good twelve feet up.

A woman sprang onto the lower line, her arms outstretched to steady herself. She looked so graceful and beautiful as she moved across it, must have felt like there wasn't a thing in the world she couldn't do, which was what fueled Syl's fascination: that idea of fearlessness: she saw it as the croon of the artist: much like a tightrope walker, the artist had to balance on a tiny line and defy expectations.

This idea was becoming increasingly important to Syl, especially as her art show was set to debut this Friday at Damascus. See, she was of the opinion that if you were going to fail as an artist, then you should fail miraculously, conspicuously. It reminded her of the guy in the 1970s who had strung a high wire between the World Trade Towers (back when there were World Trade Towers, back when America's empire was just starting to collapse). She'd watched a documentary on him and was immediately struck by the danger in his art. The stakes were mortal for him. One misjudged step or a change in wind and he was dead. How could she hold her art to the same sort of hazardous standard?

Inspiration had struck on Mission Street, as she walked by the fish market between 23rd and 24th. If not the worst smelling fish market in town, certainly cracking the top three. The smell of death was so pungent. And it dawned on her that her paintings of dead soldiers weren't enough. This was what her art had been missing. Yeah, she'd use dead fish to hammer her point home. If she was going to string her high wire, didn't she want it between the Towers, hundreds of feet in the air, where one wrong step would mean the end of her?

Now a woman's voice startled Syl as she sat in the park, sipping her latte. It was coming from the lady standing on the wire. Her arms were still outstretched, slowly moving across it. She had a big smile on her face. "Wouldn't you rather try it yourself than just watch?"

"What?"

"I can teach you how to do this."

"I'd break my neck."

"No," she said, "you won't." She pointed at the other wire, way up the tree. "You don't learn with it up there. You start down here and inch your way up."

Syl waved to her. "No thanks."

"You can't get hurt falling from here. Come on."

It made Syl wonder whether all the failed, botched, ridiculous projects throughout her twenties were the equivalent of inching up, slowly gaining confidence and experience, raising the height of her wire, readying herself to harpoon America.

The woman leaped onto the ground. "I'm not taking no for an answer."

How wonderful, Syl thought, to be forced into it, to have no option but to act. She set her latte down and walked over. The woman helped Syl climb onto one end of the tightrope and promised she'd help, would hold Syl's hand the whole time.

"I've got you," the woman said. She guided Syl. There was serious wobbling but she didn't fall. She took another step and laughed, body rocking back and forth, but as long as she had the woman's hand, she could bobble across it.

"How do you feel?" the woman asked.

"My parents would laugh at me."

"Well, they're not here."

"Thank god for tiny miracles."

"Do you want to try a step by yourself?"

"I'll fall."

"So what? It's only a couple feet."

Syl smiled. "Okay." She let go of her hand and outstretched her arms. Victorious! But only for about four seconds before teetering and falling off. She felt so free.

"You're a natural," the woman said.

"Thanks."

"You lasted way longer than I did my first time."

"I want to do it again."

"Go for it."

"I want to be up there," Syl said, pointing at the higher wire, thinking of even higher ones, strung in enormous altitudes, moving across nimbly after all her practice, spectators in awe of her skill. "How long until I'm way up there?"

•••••••

That same morning, Daphne was volunteering her literary skills at 826 Valencia, helping a high school senior write his college application essay, also known as the admission essay. Unfortunately, he wouldn't budge from a god-awful barista metaphor:

I would be a great addition to your community of learned men and women. My summer job as a Starbucks barista helped prepare me for the rigors of the college experience. As a Starbucks barista, I never knew what to expect from the next order, which is very much how real life comes at you. Maybe you think a customer is going to order a Caramel Macchiato, yet they decide on an Iced Caffè Mocha or a Cinnamon Dolce Crème Frappuccino®. A smart education can give you the powers of improvisation that all grownups need to roll with the punches in the deep end of human existence. Life is full of surprises, and I want to be a prepared, responsible Barista of the Real World.

"How can you ever be prepared for surprises?" Daph asked him, rewording the same question she'd been badgering him with. She wasn't supposed to write the essay for him, an age-old tradition that was unfortunately frowned upon at 826 with their emphasis that the kids actually do their own work (go figure). Though as a "barista of the real world" herself, wasn't Daphne qualified to let him know how stupid he sounded?

"It's like an earthquake kit," William said. "You're prepared that surprises can happen. Your flashlight is totally charged along with some cans of soup and a blanket and a battery-powered radio."

Well, at least she'd gotten him to cut the line about how the campus had "good vibes" and "tasty spots" to play Frisbee.

"Do you see how you're mixing your metaphors?" she asked him.

"Exactly. Thanks. Mix 'em up. That's how life is anyway, right? All the action coming at you nonstop."

"No, mixing them is bad."

"Why? Being a life-barista is like an earthquake kit," William said. "The more, the merrier. It totally works."

"What's the thesis of your essay?"

"Life is a crazy business, and so is being a Starbucks barista. You never know what's coming down the pike."

As she'd walked to 826 that morning, Daph had bumped into an ex, lots of her former girlfriends lurking around the Mission. Daph categorized herself as a monogamist, wanting to partner up and check that off the to-do list for good. Her relationships tended to blaze white-hot from the start, brilliantly burning beginnings that lost all flame after a couple months. Unfortunately—and here was the downside to her all-in style of monogamy—by the time things flickered and died, the women were living in Daph's apartment.

Not that she and her ex's breakup was without aplomb, no way, but seeing this one wasn't high on Daphne's list of priorities, especially when she'd written poetry till four a.m. and looked like shit. William was too young to get that you couldn't prep for every emergency because there were too many kinds of them, too many degrees and variables and ranks, some as simple as running smack into a gorgeous woman who you'd dumped because she watched too much TV and never cracked a book.

Daph faked a smile and said to her ex, "How are you?"

The ex slowed her stride but didn't stop walking. "I'm still your intellectual inferior, if that's what you mean."

Okay, so maybe the breakup wasn't coated entirely in aplomb.

Now Daph asked William, "That's your essay's thesis: you never know what's coming so be ready for everything?"

"I'm nailing this, right?" he said, smiling, chocolate in his braces.

"I think it needs a lot of work."

He looked skeptical. "Are you sure you know what you're doing?"

"I'm a published poet," she said.

"So what?"

"With an MFA."

"What's that?"

"You can't plan for everything."

"But we should totally try," William said.

"How can you plan for the unexpected?"

"To a barista of the world, the unexpected is expected."

Daph fought the urge to scream, rip her hair, claw her eyes, strangle herself. Here he was dispatching wisdom about how to mitigate emergencies and he couldn't be bothered to swish some water and get the chocolate out of those rancid braces.

Mercifully, that was when Owen walked in. Bless her uncle and his perfect timing. He wore the Santa suit and carried a to-go tray with three hot chocolates. He approached and said, "Any hard workers need a sugar fix?"

"Thanks," Daph said. "This is William."

"Hi, William, I'm Owen, Daphne's uncle."

"Time to wash your jacket, Santa," William said.

"Watch the mouth," Daphne said, "or no hot chocolate."

"Sorry," said William.

"No offense taken," Owen said. "Here," and he handed the kid a hot chocolate. "How's the work coming, you two?"

"We're still futzing out some kinks," Daph said.

"Can I hear?"

William read the whole essay to him. Daphne hoped her uncle didn't say anything too harsh or disparaging; he spent so much time bantering with drunks that he might forget how vulnerable kids could be. But then Owen clapped and said, "Well done. I like how you tie your job into it. That's smart. I'm sort of a barista myself."

You had to admire Owen's giving heart. It was like that night they had met Byron Settles—how her uncle immediately wanted to help him, while Daph's instinct was to turn the other cheek, pretend Byron wasn't there begging for clean breath. She didn't understand why a woman hadn't snatched Owen up long ago, until she thought of him sleeping on a pool table at the bar. This detail rubbed her the wrong way, and since he'd told her of it, Daph stewed plans to minimize these sad sleepovers.

"You should tell her how smart it is," William said, pointing at Daph. "She thinks it's dumb."

"I don't think it's dumb," she said.

"She said I mix my metaphors."

"I probably do, too," Owen said. "We all have our crosses to bear." He winked at William, who said, "You're pretty cool."

"Us baristas of the world gotta stick together," Owen said.

"Why are you dressed like that?"

If Daphne had been helping Owen write his admission essay, it would be about self-acceptance. This thesis she could clearly state: don't be so hard on yourself. There was no reason to be running around town like Santa Claus. Be my amazing uncle, nothing more.

"Do you like my threads?" Owen said to William.

He nodded, grinned his chocolate-braces, and said, "It's a tasty look."

"You should tell her that for me. She thinks my outfit is dumb."

"Really?" William asked.

"That's the sense I get," Owen said to William, smiled at his niece.

"Let's take a break," Daph said, and William was up and running from the table with his hot chocolate.

"He seems fun," Owen said.

"Baristas of the world?"

"Don't be a snob."

"I've never said one negative thing about your Santa costume."

"You don't have to say it; I used to change your diapers."

"And someday I'll change yours," Daph said. "Do you work tonight?"

"I'm off."

"What's your plan?"

"No plan."

"Let's go to dinner. My treat."

"Dinner, yes. Your treat, no," he said.

She could help William. She'd wear him down, appointment by appointment until his essay was pitch-perfect. They could keep his barista metaphor, just needed to approach it in a different way. She had ideas that would help. Yes, she was a snob, but she knew how to use her powers of pretense for good. Despite what her TV-addicted ex might say to the contrary.

She'd help Owen, too. He was just as important as the next person. Deserved the standard fare of self-esteem. A good admission might be something as simple as reserving the right to be nice to yourself.

machines that ache in their c: drives

There were other things happening in the world, of course. British Prime Minister Tony Blair, who had told the press that history would forgive the United States and Great Britain despite the fact there were no Weapons of Mass Destruction in Iraq, now sat alone on a veranda and openly wept for deceiving his people. (That same night, George W. Bush slept soundly, immune to any tremors of conscience.) A computer programmer in Delhi, incredibly sleep deprived and jacked on a pot-and-a-half of coffee, could have sworn his laptop whispered to him, "Maybe you should go outside." A housewife won a chili cook-off in South Carolina with a recipe she'd enhanced with cannabis. In São Paulo, a young woman fought off an attacker using jiu-jitsu and held him in an excruciating *juji-gatame* (armbar) for twelve minutes until police arrived. In Arkansas, a nine-year-old boy "borrowed" the neighbor's sedan and took police on a high speed chase covering three states. That same veteran we talked about earlier, Sam, who'd been freed from the drunk tank none the wiser about how he'd broken his nose, now had some big ridiculous cowboy by the hair and was pulling his hand back, not to punch the inbred fella, no, that would end things too quickly, just planning on slapping him, stretching this out a bit, nursing the chaos. Young siblings in Iceland constructed their first snowman. A downtrodden father of five in Edinburgh couldn't handle another day without his wife—*how could she vanish after we vowed our lives to each other?*—and in some deluded, terrible sense of problem solving, drove his children to the middle of a local bridge and threw each of them into the water.

········

Before they'd split up, Shambles burst into their bathroom one night and said to her husband, "We were madly in love. Couldn't keep our hands to ourselves. What happened to us?"

This was it. This her stand to make him see they'd devolved into snippy, sexless roommates. What was the point of being in a relationship if it was lonelier than being single?

"Did you think we'd swoon forever?" he asked.

"I did."

"I wish you would have shared your drugs."

"Please don't joke."

"But I like drugs." He was laughing.

"I'm not happy."

"This is what I expected marriage to be like."

"Why don't you care?" she said.

"After eight years, I still have something left to prove to you?"

"After eight years, yes."

"I could have gone to medical school in less time than that, and they'd have trusted me with people's lives."

"No jokes," she said.

"I'm not joking."

"You were trusted with our lives."

"Don't be so dramatic."

"Do you remember when we went to Jenner?" she asked.

"Where?"

"That town up the coast. Where the Russian River meets the ocean."

"I don't think so."

"Then you probably don't remember our feet," Shambles said.

"I haven't seen my feet in years. Remind me."

"No," she said, because telling him would be too pitiful. Reliving it would remind her of all she'd ignored that day. The warning.

As newlyweds, they had gone north from San Francisco for a romantic weekend. The beach was the site of that rare collision between fresh and salt water, Russian River living up to its homophone and barreling toward the ocean. The beach wasn't too crowded. Couples paired off. Parents watching kids build castles or chase seagulls or write their names with crooked sticks or skipping rocks. One boy put a huge piece of seaweed on his head, arms outstretched in front of him and groaning like a monster.

It was fall. Overcast. Four surfers sitting on their boards and rubbing their cold shoulders through wetsuits.

Shambles and her husband had come as the tide was out, ocean occupying much less of the beach than normal. Because of the velocity that carried the Russian River toward the ocean, it gouged a two-foot trench in the beach that spanned about thirty feet across. People couldn't get by it. Standing on one side or the other and watching the water's authority as it yanked more sand from the sides of the trench, widening the gap. Of course, as the tide came up again, it would rearrange the beach's sand and the trench would vanish, smoothed over. But for now, this part of the beach was impassable.

They walked up to the trench's edge, watched sand continue to crumble from the lips. Sloughing in huge clumps. A heap slipped into the water right in front of them, and Shambles took a step backward.

"Don't," her husband said.

"What?"

"Stay here," he said, and with his shoe etched a line parallel to the edge. "Let's see how long until it deteriorates this far." He aligned his toes perfectly with it. "How long do you think until it reaches us?"

She sighed and stepped up to the line. Silent. Eyes fixed down at the crumbling sand.

"Come on, what's your guess?" he asked.

"I don't know."

"I'll say one minute," he said, and they were quiet. No other words to speak. Just the rush of the river barreling. The sound of slopping sand peeling and plopping into the water. A rogue squawk from a gull. Wind. Waves crashing.

"Should we wager on who's right?" her husband said, sticking his hand out for a shake to seal the stakes of their arrangement, but why, Shambles thought, why should we gamble on how fast the world would whittle away?

All she said was this: "Let's just wait and see."

He retracted his hand, disappointed.

Thirty seconds later, the ground gave way.

•••••••

Once they separated, Shambles found herself in some other Mission District dive bar than Damascus and struck up a conversation with a cute, young guy and the more they drank the crasser the conversation turned and soon they were talking about what they'd do to one another right there at the bar and he said, "Wow, I'm getting hard just talking this way," and she said, "That's what I like to hear," and they were talking about going back to his place and making it official, but he wanted to cum now, please, jerk me off. So they were up and in the bathroom. The act was over quickly, and once he'd been wiped clean and she'd washed her hands, they bellied back up to the bar for a celebratory whiskey.

"You're a riot," he said. "I guess it's time to settle up."

"Huh?"

"How much is your fine hospitality gonna run me?"

She knew what he meant, what he assumed about her, and she wasn't the slightest bit offended. Okay, fine, sure, she was probably the slightest bit offended, but what were her options in the moment? Either she laughed it off or threw a temper tantrum. Both were just shields from his hypothesis, bulletproof vests. She was drunk and nursing her marriage's failure and flexing her sexuality, the power in it, the yearn she could elicit in men with the promise of orgasm. Why had her husband lost all interest in touching her? Why had the eroticism emigrated from their life? What had changed? And why weren't there ever any answers to questions like these, the ones that really needed them?

Seeing as how the hand job was already on the books, no reason, she decided, to keep him from bequeathing the bar tab. "How does forty bucks sound?"

"Fair enough. Nice doing business with you," he said and paid her.

"You still want to go back to your place?"

"No thanks."

"But what about my needs?" she said, trying to flirt. "A woman has bodily needs, too, young man."

"Sorry."

That question—*what about my needs?*—might be her mantra.

The guy got up and left and Shambles drank his forty dollar donation before an hour had elapsed.

•••••••

Vamping hard at a thirty-two-year-old something or other. He was vague about his job. Computers? A baby face, breath that reeked of hummus. Shambles didn't care. She was seducing him. She had so much sexual clout with these men. They begged her. They'd have done anything to get off. They needed her. She said, "Would you like me to make you cum?" and he said, "Yes," and she said, "Let's go to the bathroom," and when they loped back to the bar, ol' bad-breath-baby-face offered to pay her.

The figure she'd told the first fellow made as much sense as any of this. "Forty's fine," she said, this time not asking if there was any interest in getting her off, too. She was quickly learning that wasn't the point.

·········

And the next time she just came right out and laid the stakes. This one was middle-aged. A limo driver. Told her that his ride was out front of Damascus and they could fool around in the back like celebrities, but she felt safer doing it in the bar's bathroom (not yet known as her office), which disappointed him but she didn't care.

This was the first time she articulated any rules, though they were pared down to the gaudy bone: "Don't cum on me." She aimed the early ones at the toilet, though it never worked and she ended up cleaning the floors, a throwback to one of her past lives, swabbing the base of toilets at the assisted living facility.

Although it occurred to her that a bar was its own kind of assisted living facility.

·········

It became part of her life, her routine. A jerk here, one there. A nice way to subsidize happy hour. And it was so much quicker than going to her crappy job. Do a couple a night. No big deal. So she quit. No notice. Just stopped going. She had her new gig, one for which there would always be a demand, always at least a couple lonely pervs in a bar. But she was usually doing at least three a night and making enough dough to tread water. To keep treading water.

She had her own office and her universe was shrinking. Leashed into a small yard. A dog guarding a vacant lot, guarding nothing. Much like Owen, there were days Shambles never went any place besides her apartment and Damascus.

Careful what you wish for: she was way outside the borders of monogamy. She was in the worst kind of confinement now. And didn't know it.

·········

Waking him up after he'd dozed on the toilet in Damascus's bathroom, Shambles said to No Eyebrows, "We need to get out of here."

He yawned, pulled his head up from the wall and asked, "Did someone knock?"

"No, but Owen doesn't like it when I'm in here too long."

He pulled his pants up. She leaned her face down to the sink, drank some water, gargled, spat.

"Would you like another whiskey?" No Eyebrows said.

"A drink sounds good."

They walked toward the bar. No Eyebrows gazed up and noticed Owen's new clouds; he nudged Shambles and said, "Those things are atrocious."

"Owen's trying new things."

"I'm all in favor of that." He pointed at a particularly crude rendition. "I've just never seen a cloud that says Corona on its side."

Shambles laughed. "Okay, I'll give you that one."

He ordered shots of schnapps and whiskey. "What should we drink to?" hoisting his glass up high.

Shambles brought hers up to his level. Smiled at him. There was something weird welling inside her. What they'd done in the bathroom—what she'd done in the bathroom—had never happened before. There was no commerce in that moment. There was only intimacy. He'd named his first tumor after his daughter, and all Shambles wanted to do in the moment was make him feel good, better, whatever. Shambles wanted to help him. She never thought of these deadbeats as real people with real lives, stories stretching into their pasts. She didn't want to hear anybody's sob story. But this was different. He broke her no-touching rule, his fingers rubbing her back, and she liked it. Damnit, she liked it! No Eyebrows was different. That first night she couldn't resist the urge to look in his eyes and they'd had that wonderful hug and now she'd given him a blowjob and wanted more. She was feeling something. She was feeling again.

So she said to him, "Let's drink to our first date."

"Really?"

"Yeah. Let's finish these and get out of here."

It was one a.m. and had started to pour rain. The gutter in front of the bar wasn't draining well, jammed with cardboard, old clothing, newspapers. Water collected on the street in a big puddle. The traffic lights in front of Damascus blinked red. A homeless man scurried by using a to-go box as an umbrella. Another guy without any kind of makeshift shield stood in front of a mailbox and knocked violently on its rounded blue body, shouting, "I'm not leaving until you answer my damn questions, Victor! You hear me? I've got all night."

A taxi approached. No Eyebrows stuck his hand up, but as it got closer he noticed there was someone in the back.

"I'm not really that hungry," Shambles said. "Are you?"

He shrugged. "Not for months." She looked away from him.

He still hadn't gotten used to people's reactions, whenever he brought up his illness. People seemed ready to talk about Cancer, capital-*C*: what type is it, what stage, what kind of chemo? But no one liked cancer, small-*c*: the vicious ubiquities: never being hungry, always freezing, losing the feeling in your feet, losing your motor skills, vertigo, nausea, hating loud noise, being feeble—so damn feeble.

No Eyebrows kept his arm craned up in the air and finally a cab approached. "I used to love driving in the rain," he said to her.

"Then why are you hailing a cab?"

"We'll let someone else do the work. We can talk."

"Do you have money?"

"That's one thing I have plenty of."

They hopped in the cab while the soaked man stood at the mailbox, pleading with Victor to come on out and answer his questions; No Eyebrows said to the driver, "Will you just meander around for a while?"

The man nodded. He'd been smoking in the cab with the windows rolled up. The cabbie was having a tough night—freshly removed from having his boyfriend tell him to save up first and last months' rent and vacate their apartment, their affinity, as quickly as possible.

"Where am I going to get that kind of money?" he'd asked him.

"Last time I checked," the boyfriend said, "blood and semen were going for top dollar. I know you've got the latter, though I have no idea what pumps through that heart of yours."

Now the cabbie asked Shambles and No Eyebrows, "Any particular neighborhood you want me to end up in?"

"Back here. Eventually," No Eyebrows said. He put his hand out and Shambles took it. She thought about how cold his was; he thought, please touch me till the end of time.

"You mind if I smoke?" the driver asked them.

"I already have lung cancer," No Eyebrows said, "but you better check with this lovely lady."

She shook her head. "I have bigger problems than second-hand smoke."

The cabbie lit up, wove around the Mission District, down 24th Street to Potrero, past Walgreen's and SF General. The roads empty because of the downpour.

"Are you married?" No Eyebrows said to Shambles.

"I was. You?"

"Married. Yes. With a little girl."

"Where are they?"

"Still in my old life."

"Where are you?"

"Here," said No Eyebrows, cramping with smoggy guilt but trying to ignore it. He looked out the windshield and couldn't see where they were going, raindrops pelting and pelting. The wiper blades seemed old to him, useless. He didn't know how the driver saw the road, and he didn't really care, holding her hand.

"When did you leave?" she said.

"Do you know anything about World War I?" he asked.

Shambles shook her head. The cab took 17th up toward Potrero Hill.

No Eyebrows said, "So many soldiers and civilians died in Germany that the orphanages were crammed with children. A lot of them babies. There were so many of them that the nurses and nuns and workers did their best to give all the children some attention, but it was impossible. There were just too many. There are stories about workers losing their minds, listening to the babies wail at the same time. Can you imagine hearing all those helpless squeals? Can you imagine trying to do your part but no matter what you did, it wasn't enough, there was always another mewling baby? The workers fed and changed them. They did everything they had time to do. They gave their all. But the babies needed to be picked up; they needed to be held. A lot of them died because nobody had time to give them any affection."

The cab's windows fogged so the driver turned on the defroster. He kept weaving quickly up a series of residential streets. Turned left at the next block and as the road dipped down into a small valley, it was flooded, rainwater too high to go on. He turned the car around, said, "We'll have to try the next one," but neither person in the backseat responded.

"People think they have everything figured out," No Eyebrows said to Shambles. "It embarrasses me to remember how much ego I had. Do you know I actually drove a Porsche? Ever heard the joke about the difference between a cactus and a Porsche? A cactus has its prick on the outside." He scoffed. "That was me: I was the prick in the Porsche in my designer suits: how humiliating: I'm a cliché, a cautionary tale.

"If I had it to do over again, I wouldn't save anything. Not a penny tucked away, no secret accounts, no just-in-case contingencies. I wouldn't fantasize about what to do during my retirement. I'd take my wife around the globe. I'd buy a map and cross off each country we visited, and we'd keep traveling until we'd seen everything. Until we knew what the whole world was like."

Yes, they should have seen it all. Their passports should have been worn dockets of their adventures. Instead, here was No Eyebrows weaving aimlessly around San Francisco in a taxi, all that potential and planning and future swept up and heaved in an incinerator. And his wife Sally was weaving in another way, wondering where he was, what he was doing. He should call her. He should email. He should send a card to his daughter. He should act like a god damn man, but he wasn't one, he was a corpse. Disease was the world they'd see together. That lone malignant stamp in their passport.

His throat was dry, voice getting fainter as the rant pushed on: "And I'd spoil Erica to a preposterous degree. Shameless pampering. Why not? What reason is there to be sensible?" He snapped his fingers. "My whole life disappeared. It ended, and the worst part is, I'm still alive. I have to watch my own death. I never thought my life would end until I was ready. I'd go out at ninety-four, surrounded by my wife and daughter and grand-children and maybe even a great-grandchild. That's the ending I was convinced I'd get. Convinced I *deserved*. Why did I get this ending? Why me?"

"Nobody gets to choose," she said.

"Where's the reason in it?"

"There isn't any."

"We're all machines," he said. "Temporary machines. Useless and dying ones with heavy egotistical hearts. Machines that ache in our c: drives."

He mentioned hearts, and Shambles thought about his, stretched with anger and lamentations, the way a snake bulged after swallowing a rodent whole. And all the hopefulness she'd felt as they left Damascus was turning to ash, much like the driver's cigarette. What if she had been wrong and he wasn't supposed to save her... what if she was supposed to be the hero, supposed to disarm the dynamite that had been strapped to his chest by terrorists? What if she was supposed to magically remove his tumors?

The cab made a couple more quick turns, and they came to another flooded intersection. This time the driver was able to cross it with two wheels on the sidewalk.

"That first night, when you offered to touch me," No Eyebrows said, "I knew you did it to other men, but at that specific second, you only wanted to put your hands on me. You chose me."

"I don't know what to say."

"Tell me what you're thinking."

"I can't."

"Please?"

The next intersection was flooded, too. They couldn't go forward.

"What should I do?" the cabbie asked, but neither answered him; he put the car in park, idling. He was ingesting No Eyebrows' words, imagining himself alone in a new apartment, away from his boyfriend, without anyone to touch his skin. He lit a new cigarette on the butt of the other.

No Eyebrows reached over and rubbed Shambles' spine; she let him do it, but it didn't make her feel any affection, as it had earlier in her office. She should have stayed in Damascus. Her rules were there for a reason.

"I'm the only child of two only children," No Eyebrows said. "I left my wife and daughter. I need to feel alive again."

"Can't go on," the cabbie said, voice growing more impatient.

"Will you come back to my hotel room tonight?" No Eyebrows asked her. "I'll pay you whatever. Please sleep with me. Please be in the same bed and let me feel your warm body."

She stared out the fogged window, used a finger to clear some moisture away so she could see outside.

"Please do this for me," No Eyebrows said.

Nothing, no words, only her finger on the cold window, etching patterns.

"I'm still alive," he said.

Shambles drew a curlicue on the glass, a claustrophobic shape closing in on itself.

"Please come with me," he begged her, "please."

Her finger reached the center of the curlicue. Trapped. She pulled it off the glass at the center of the shape because there was nowhere else to go. He wasn't asking her to sleep in his bed. He was asking for a miracle.

"I can't save you," Shambles said.

"That's not what I want."

"Yes, it is."

"No."

"I can't. I'm sorry."

Silence.

Carnivorous, cancerous silence.

"We'll have to go back the way we came," the cabbie said and put the car in reverse.

night owl slumber party

Owen and Byron Settles were having a slumber party after Damascus closed, each crashed out on one of the pool tables and squirreled away in sleeping bags. Owen lit a couple candles and placed them on the bar, making the stars on the ceiling twinkle. Both men were on their backs, staring straight up.

"This is sort of like camping," Byron said.

"I can think of a few minor differences."

"I love camping. Reminds me of being a boy."

"The most major difference being that we're inside," said Owen. He had stripped out of his Santa suit to sleep; Byron was in his underwear, too. On the edge of each man's pool table was a fig bar that Owen had picked up special for them, though Byron couldn't figure out why.

"Don't rain on my camping-parade," Byron Settles said. "My dad used to take me all the time. He was a minister. They say the apple doesn't fall far from the tree, but I landed worlds away from him."

"How's your fig bar?" Owen asked, chomping on his. He expected Byron to have devoured it right away. If there was one thing Owen remembered from Daph being a little girl, she never left any snacks out on Christmas Eve for Santa Claus that she didn't love herself, hoping he might not be able to chow down everything and leave some pieces behind. So if fig bars were what Byron baked and left out, seemed like a safe bet they were his favorite.

"I don't like those things."

"I thought you used to make them."

"Not me."

"That's what you told me the first night we met."

"I was in a blackout," said Byron. "That's one thing I do have in common with my dad: I lie when I drink."

Owen didn't want to talk about fathers, felt too old to possess such a calloused grudge against his old man, but sometimes our rusted memories maintained their extraordinary architecture. He wasn't going to allow any unscheduled trips down memory lane tonight, wanted to enjoy entertaining his guest. Some people might call a couple guys encased in sleeping bags on pool tables depressing, but Owen didn't see it that way at all. He was having a blast and wanted to keep the mood light, so he pointed at the ceiling and said, "Did you see that?"

"See what?"

"A shooting star."

Byron played along. "I think I did."

"I guess we both get wishes then."

"You first."

"I want to meet a woman," Owen said. "An old woman. With baggage. One who has a lot of flaws and won't dwell on mine. And not too pretty. But she's nice. And might consider having sex with me a couple times."

"Covered all your bases. Very shrewd."

"Thanks. What's yours?"

"I want to go home," Byron Settles said. "I'm back, but I'm not home. There's a difference."

Both of them felt a sense of calm, swaddled on the pool tables. Getting sleepy. Some of it was drunkenness, sure, but to say that was everything would belittle their camaraderie. They were comfortable. Owen was excited for the company, and Byron appreciated the break from all his problems. He'd stopped pining for what his life used to look like, abandoned all possibility that you could tunnel back into earlier versions of yourself. There were flukes, disasters, and then there were the consequences of these events, and that was your new life.

"Did you call your wife again?" Owen asked.

"Tried, but she sent me to voicemail."

"Better than sending you away for good. Me and you can camp out a few more nights if you want."

"She may not let me come back this time."

"This time?"

"She's requested I temporarily vacate the premises before."

"It'll be fine."

"I'm a bad person," Byron said. "Big temper. You should know that about me."

"I don't believe it."

"And I wish that changed something, but I'm still the same bad man."

They went quiet for a couple minutes, staring up at Damascus's planetarium, the wavering constellations of man-made stars. Owen racked his mind for the right words. He wanted to say something about empathy, wanted to tell Byron that he understood. He was a bad person, too. Every time Owen swallowed a sip of a cocktail he'd promised not to pour. Every time he woke with a hangover, wondering what kept him living, and why, since he contributed nothing to the world. So even if he and Byron had sovereign reasons for branding themselves bad, they shared the same shame, funneling the last drops of self-hate like a drunkard sucking booze through a cracked straw, working so hard for so little.

All that damn stewing for one damn answer and Owen couldn't come up with anything so he went with this: "I saw another shooting star!"

Byron smiled. "Where?"

"Above the jukebox. This one was really bright."

"I missed it," Byron said, "but you still get another wish."

"I'll stick with my original. No need to get greedy."

"In the Corps, I was a paramarine. Used to streak like a shooting star."

"Really?"

"No better feeling than before you pull the cord, man."

"Were you in Iraq?"

"I tried to be," Byron Settles said. "I wanted to be. Trained my whole life for it. But my knee shredded on my landing in-country."

"That's awful."

"Like I said, I'm back, but I can't find my way home. No matter if I blow in my steering wheel or not." His wife kept talking about his temper since he'd been home. He'd burned garlic and spiked the pan on the floor. He yelled at a teenage worker at McDonalds for forgetting his fries. Put his fist through the passenger window of their car, sitting in a traffic jam. "This isn't like you," she said, and he said, "Must be. I'm the one doing it." And she wanted him to quit drinking, take anger management classes, go to counseling, do something. "Come back to me," was how she'd end these pleas.

She was probably right about the booze, the counseling, but lots of people were probably right about lots of things, didn't mean nothing to Byron right then. Not while he drifted down from the highest jump of his life, falling, no landing zone anywhere in sight. She couldn't make him care, couldn't give him a direct order, though often Byron wished someone would. He'd found a freedom in the Corps, the organization, the structure, no gray areas. You always knew where you stood, and what you were standing on.

He shook these ideas out of his head. It was his turn to lighten things up: "I saw a shooting star, too. Over by the bathroom."

"Good eye. Want another wish?"

"Might as well. I need all the help I can get."

"The jury's still out on you."

If there was a jury chewing Byron's case, they'd see right through him and know his heart had turned like rotting meat. He changed the subject: "Do you know what we look like right now?"

"What?"

"With our heads sticking out of the sleeping bags, we look like bagel dogs. A couple drunken bagel dogs."

Owen got a good chuckle. "I'm taking that as a compliment."

"How else can you take it, man?"

The two of them kept laughing before settling down for a night's rest. Byron snored like nobody Owen had ever heard, but he didn't care, stargazing and enjoying the company of this stray, a lost dog just like Owen. A couple castoffs doing their best, even if it only lasted until Byron's wife came to the pound to pick him up and left Owen alone again in his black-walled cage. Friendship didn't have to last long, if it sutured some gash of loneliness you might otherwise bleed out from. People could stitch one another up and move on. Transient, merciful surgeons knotting susceptible skin.

•••••••

Owen dreamed of a frantic woman, Byron's wife, running down a city street and stapling flyers to telephone poles:

Lost Bagel Dog
Answers to Byron Settles
Last Seen Blowing into a Steering Wheel and
Trying to Get Back Home.

•••••••

But Byron wasn't having the same quick-drying affection as his counterpart. Sure, some lost dogs slaked for love and leaped into a stranger's arms, oblivious to danger, but others had learned that life was full of molesters and devils. These dogs bared fangs for every treacherous lesson the world had taught them: trust got you nowhere, except kicked in the kidneys.

So yes, Byron was sleeping in a strange place, but he felt safe at Damascus, at ease—no chance he couldn't whup a sixty-year-old Santa Claus. He didn't need two good knees to do that. He wasn't even worried about it, focusing on bunking down and hoping his wife decided to give him another chance. One he didn't deserve, hadn't earned. He tried not to think about it from her perspective. That was where indignity lived. That was torture.

Play the hand you're dealt, said the mean cliché, but how could we even want to play a game so obviously fixed for us to lose?

• • • • • • • •

He woke up before Owen. Still drunk. One of the candles on the bar was lit, but barely, flickering and making a hissing noise, about to go out for good. What time was it? He guessed about four a.m. Still dark.

Byron Settles moved behind the bar for a glass of water, but once back there, man, oh, man that Hennessy bottle drove a hard bargain. No reason he couldn't kill two liquid birds. Big shot of Hennessy, then a pint of water.

He noticed the cash register, thought about seeing if it was worth robbing. What kind of douchebag robbed a guy who was helping you? His finger fumbled over the old-time buttons, paused over No Sale. One more shot of Hennessy.

That was when the candle conked out and Damascus went pitch black.

• • • • • • • •

Owen must have been the second bagel dog to come to because as he looked around the bar from his sleeping bag, Byron's was already empty and lay crumpled on the pool table. His fig bar was untouched and on the table's railing. Owen stretched, climbed into his Santa suit. He knew that an aspirin was in his immediate future and stumbled toward his stash behind the bar. The cash register was open. Money was still in the till, but it wasn't like him to leave it like that: on nights too liquored to hit the safe, he at least closed the drawer as protection, which was like leaving your dead bolt open but latching that flimsy, ridiculous chain as fortification; only thing that would help you any less should a robber come calling was prayer.

Pushing the drawer closed, Owen tried to wash down an aspirin, but it sort of stuck in his throat. Then he heard the bar's toilet flush and he filled with relief, glad the lost dogs were still a pack.

Byron veered out and said, "I'm not normally a morning yacker. Hope I'm not pregnant."

"We didn't go all the way," said Owen. "Your virtue is safe."

"I need some food to settle my stomach."

"Eat your fig bar."

"Nah. Wanna get breakfast?"

"The fig bars are good."

"And I need to buy a toothbrush."

Owen could feel the aspirin caught in his throat. Breathing was fine, but the pill was plastered in there. He should take another swig of water to wash it down. "We'll get whatever you need."

"But first I'm going to yack again," Byron said. "Don't know what's come over me."

"Best of luck."

"Not much luck involved, really. Just try not to dribble puke on yourself. It's like riding a bike: once you've got it dialed in, you're all good."

Owen shook his head playfully and said, "Only you would think puking and bike riding is the same thing."

Byron had been walking toward the bathroom, but he stopped moving once he heard Owen's words. He was uneasy with the way Owen spoke. As if they had history. Civilian life was its own kind of Corps, one he hadn't been trained to function in.

"Only I'd say that?" he said to Owen. "You don't even know me, remember?"

"I'm a good judge of character."

"Not really."

Owen coughed, tried to swallow a wad of spit to budge the pill, but no luck. "Honest. Bartenders meet a lot of jerks, thugs, you name it. You're one of the good guys. I can tell."

"You got me all wrong," Byron said. "I'm a whole other monster."

Owen was still coughing. "Says who?"

"Everybody that's known me more than a week." Then Byron went into the bathroom and got sick again.

Owen listened to him retch and finally rinsed the stuck pill down. Last thing he did was walk over and eat Byron's fig bar. Erase the evidence. It wasn't a big deal if he'd lied about something as silly as dessert. But still, Owen wanted to chew it up and send it chasing after that aspirin. Felt pretty stupid letting somebody crash on your pool table and buying them fig bars if they weren't being honest with you. Better to chalk it up to a blacked-out first impression. Could have happened to anybody, right?

the harry potter debacle

It was too surreal for Syl to keep secret: how in the midst of another one-night stand a couple weeks back, the man looked up at her as Syl bounced on top of him, her flat chest, circle-rimmed glasses, short stringy brown hair, and he said, "You look just like Harry Potter. Holy smokes, it's like I'm nailing Harry Potter, and it's totally turning me on, man."

She was currently recounting the Harry Potter Debacle to her best friend, Daphne, and Owen, who for some reason was wearing a Santa Claus costume blotted with liquor stains. Also present was a gentleman named Byron Settles. If Syl understood the story correctly, he'd been bunking on one of Damascus's pool tables this week while he and his wife ironed out a squabble over him "accidentally" detouring to San Francisco and binge drinking.

"I'm super handy with a broom," Byron had told Syl as they first shook hands. "I'm earning my keep around here. No hand-outs for this cadet. I'm serious about that."

"What's his keep?" Syl said to Owen.

"Almost a bottle of Hennessy a night. Not sure I'm getting the better end of the deal."

Byron pretended to push a broom, *maniacally* pushing the unseen broom. "I'm an artist with this thing. I'd eat off these floors. Breakfast, lunch, and dinner. I'd deliver a baby on 'em."

Syl supposed his assertion that he'd eat off the floor would be true regardless of its cleanliness. He was in desperate need of a good night's rest. Eyes bloodshot with a splotchy beard and hair matted into fronds. It surprised Syl to hear that he and Owen had just met, considering they acted like bosom chums (at least Owen acted the part); it was nice of Owen to offer him a place to stay. But it was weird, wasn't it? Yes, people were supposed to help one another. Syl knew this. More often than not it seemed to work out exactly the opposite, people pretending the evidence of others' travesties weren't speckled all over their faces like open sores.

This was to be Syl's first public showing, so even though she didn't think Damascus was an ideal site, she had to make lemonade out of these desperate lemons. Fact was Syl needed some gusto, something positive to happen to remind her why she toiled so hard on her artwork though no one in the world seemed to give a shit. Some days *she* didn't even give a shit, wondered how anyone else was supposed to enjoy your stuff if even you struggled to see its merits. But that was before the dead fish, her extraordinary idea, before she envisioned herself walking the high wire, totally prepared for the challenge and ready to bare her inspired soul.

It was early afternoon. The task at hand—which hadn't started yet—was to hang Syl's paintings on the walls for the opening that evening. What was actually transpiring was a round of whiskeys with beer-chasers.

"Harry Potter?" Owen now said to Syl. "That's pretty romantic. Are you two going to elope?"

"It's a good illustration of why I'm queer. No offense, uncle," Daph said, to which Owen wordlessly shrugged, before she added, "You too, Byron. I'm not trying to stereotype men."

"No offense taken," Byron said. "That story might make me gay, too."

They downed their whiskeys, sipped from their beers.

Up to this point, Syl's twelve paintings leaned against a wall, bundled up in old newspaper. She categorized it as an Olfactory

Installation because as the show hung for the whole month, the smell of dead fish would terrorize the patrons, reminding them of the piling American casualties, the war not even a year old yet. Or so Syl hoped.

"We will not be eloping, thank you very much," Syl said to Owen. "He said it like it was the most natural thing in the world. Like every guy fantasized about screwing Harry Potter."

Quiet...

Abject silence...

Pondering...

"Gentlemen, is it true?" Daph finally said. "Is Harry Potter a male sexual fantasy?"

"I'm staying out of this," Owen said.

Everyone's attention turned to Byron, who said with an odd, matter of fact tone, "I'm not really into wizards."

"What's wrong with wizards?" Daph sassed him.

"For one, they wear those stupid hats. How is anyone supposed to be turned on by a hat like that?"

"Anything else?"

"He's also a dude," Byron Settles said.

"Let's move on to our next topic of conversation, shall we?" Syl said. "Who wants to help me hang some paintings?"

"One more quick pop?" Byron said, a well-timed suggestion. "I'm still a little thirsty."

Owen became the center of attention, the final word on whether another whiskey was in the cards: "What kind of host would I be if I didn't offer another shot to three of my closest friends?"

He happily refilled their glasses, which seconds later were empty again.

"Smooth taste," Byron said. He had a look on his face like he was going to vomit. "Living in Damascus has been better than summer camp."

"You don't technically live here," Owen said, teasing, though he liked the idea very much, regular camping trips to lay back and stargaze.

"Semantics," said Byron. "'Where I lay my head is home.' Didn't some poet say that?"

"Metallica," Daphne said. "The poets of the mullet community."

Whiskeys finished, they all walked over to Syl's bundled paintings. The four of them stood in front of the concealed portraits, ready to tear through the newspaper like children ripping into presents. Owen, Daph, and Syl all knew what they were about to see, but Byron didn't know anything about the pictures of dead soldiers. No one had told him squat about the art show. Yeah, he knew one was happening tonight, but as to what was actually featured, he had no idea.

Until they began unwrapping them.

Until they tore through the newspaper.

Until he saw the portraits firsthand.

The four of them gawking at the pictures.

All twelve painted on plywood. You could tell they were soldiers because a couple wore helmets patterned in desert camouflage; a few had flak jackets visible; their names and ranks written across the bottoms next to the days they died. Each now leaned against the wall for perusal, lined up like they stood in some kind of formation.

Twelve casualties staring Byron Settles in the face and asking what he was doing here, did he condone this, was he really a part of something so defaming? He didn't need much help feeling as though he'd abandoned his unit. He'd jumped out of so many planes and nothing was different that time. His two-second war. He was in proper form to land, turned into the wind just right. He did everything the way he was supposed to, and his body failed him. As they were shipping him home, one superior had asked what the hell went wrong, and Byron told him it was a fluke, to which he said, "Marines don't make mistakes."

Those four words haunted Byron.

As did the words Honorable Discharge.

Because where was this stash of honor? There was no honor in letting down the guys on his left and right. No honor in all those years of training for nothing. He didn't even make it into the fight, hadn't faced down one enemy.

And now Byron, along with all his clogged animosity, stood in front of these twelve casualties. She'd turned veterans into an art project. Ripped them from the context of being heroes. She wasn't allowed to rape their memory. Hell, no. He wouldn't let them get turned into advertisements, some bullshit propaganda. They had families and friends and beyond that, they had the courage to fight. To do something. To defend our country. The country where you have the luxury of sitting on your ass and scribbling your meaningless pictures.

Maybe this was the Honorable part of his discharge. Maybe he was supposed to confront *dishonor*. Maybe his landing zone was here—behind enemy lines he hadn't even known about.

"What's the point of these pictures?" Byron said to Syl.

"The point?"

"You heard me."

"Hopefully, they're indictments."

"Of what?"

"The audience. Us. Those of us safely back in America going about our business as if soldiers aren't dying every day."

Us. Those of Us.

Four new words to torment Byron.

He couldn't believe his ears and couldn't believe his eyes and there was no such thing as *us*. Not in this context. He was a Sky Soldier, a warrior, a killer raining down, and Syl had not been authorized to speak on his behalf.

"You've got some fuckin' balls on you, lady," Byron said.

"What's wrong?" she asked.

"Who the fuck do you think you are?"

"Byron, let's me and you get some air and chat, huh?" Owen said, trying to rush him out. All those years tending bar had served Owen well in identifying this sort of blooming anger. He'd seen it many times before men punched one another, head-butted their antagonists, used empty bottles as tomahawks cracking, sometimes splitting skulls. "Come on. Let's go outside."

"You're disrespecting soldiers, bitch," Byron said to Syl. "That shit won't fly on my watch."

"It's actually all about respect for them," she said. "No one's paying attention to the war. It's not even Page One news anymore."

"They're defending you."

"Come on, Byron," Owen said. "I mean it. Let's get some air." He touched Byron lightly on the elbow and tried moving him, not aggressively, toward the door. Luckily, Byron didn't buck with him, though he did say to Syl while taking steps toward the exit, "You don't know what you're talking about, bitch!"

Syl was confused and also sort of scared. Byron had blown up out of nowhere—what if everyone saw her paintings the same way he did? What if her high wire had been strung too loosely and all that slack would lead to her demise?

Owen and Byron Settles were outside, in the midday fog. It was windy. A woman was selling Mexican wrestling masks from a shopping cart. Another carried an armful of pamphlets speaking the word of god, written in Spanish; she kept trying to hand them to people and most shook her away, unwilling, unabashed in their atheism. A man stumbled by with a big ball of dirty laundry clutched to his chest (he lost an argyle sock before reaching the Laundromat). There was a UPS truck blocking traffic in front of the bar, horns honking from the frustrated drivers stuck behind, forced to wait it out, unable to swerve around due to the consistent traffic coming in the opposite direction.

"I can't have you talking to her like that," Owen said. "You're my guest. You need to treat my niece and her friends with respect."

"I don't need to do anything."

"If you want to come back inside, yes you do."

"She's got some nerve with those pictures."

"She thinks they're important."

More blaring horns as the UPS driver loped from business to business, delivering packages.

"They're not important at all," Byron said. "They're just doodles. The people in the pictures are what's important."

"She's entitled to her opinion."

"I know they say that everyone's entitled to their opinion, but I think that's just preschool bullshit. She's wrong, real wrong. You shouldn't let her hang them."

"Why not?"

"Do you agree with her?"

"How's that matter?"

"Do you or not?"

"I don't have an opinion on the subject."

"Letting her hang them is an opinion," Byron Settles said. "A very loud fucking opinion."

"You need to calm down."

"You need to think about what you're saying by letting those paintings hang. You're telling your customers that you agree with her."

The UPS driver made his way back to the truck, started it up and rolled on, freeing the cars bottlenecked behind it.

"I like you," said Byron. "You saved my ass the other night. We're boys. But this is serious shit. You can't let her hang those."

"I know you served, but why are you taking this so personally?"

"It could be me, man. I could be hanging on your wall. Don't you get that?" he said, which wasn't the whole truth. It was one tine of it: the prospect that Byron could have died over there and been immortalized in a portrait truly bothered him. The way

Syl took soldier's faces and twisted their meaning. Not honoring their sacrifice but mocking it, loading it up like a Trojan horse, shoving its belly full of enemies. She was going to use their faces to say something against the war—a cause they believed in. It wasn't right, and they weren't here to defend themselves, but guess who was—guess who could redeem his "honorable" absence at Bashur?

But another thing wedged in his craw, too, imploded it just like his knee: Syl's assumption about *us*. Jesus, he hated being lumped in with these cowards. They had no common ground. He'd given everything to the Corps, and why was he the one whose knee locked up? Why couldn't it have been someone else's body letting down another marine? Why didn't he get the chance to do what he'd trained his whole adult life to do?

"She doesn't mean it how you're taking it," Owen said.

"It's life and death for us. It's real." Byron balled his hands into fists. "Don't let her hang them."

Owen looked at Byron's fists. "But I already agreed to let her hang them."

"Change your mind."

Fear. For the first time, Owen was afraid of Byron.

"I can't," Owen said, thinking not so much about how changing his mind and canceling the opening would affect Syl, but of disappointing Daphne. She wouldn't understand a flip of the heart based on Byron's outburst, and the idea of letting her down over someone he just met wasn't possible for Owen, even as he sweated the notion of getting punched in the face.

"Then fuck you very much," Byron Settles said. "I know that makes me sound like a bum because you let me sleep on your pool table. But if you let this bullshit hang, who knows what might happen."

"What do you mean by that?"

"Just what I said."

"Are you threatening me?" Yes, they'd been staying up late,

each wrapped in a sleeping bag and perched on pool tables, gabbing back and forth like teenage girls gossiping at a slumber party, but what if Byron was dangerous? What if he actually was a bad person, as he'd been telling Owen the whole time? There was the chance that he'd only been playing nice so far because Owen was extending himself so drastically. The chance that Owen needed to be afraid of him.

And there was also the chance that Byron was right about this: were these paintings insulting to soldiers? Owen had no idea. Syl said the portraits weren't really about the military, but the citizens back home, the audience who looked at them. How was Owen supposed to find out, figure out, who was right?

"I'm telling you that this sort of shit riles folks," Byron said. "I'm serious about that. Mark my words. I like you but this shit is too disrespectful." Then he turned and walked away.

Owen called after him, "Don't leave like this." He stood stupidly, watching him go, already missing his strange friend, this belligerent man he barely knew at all. "Don't go! Please! Let's talk! It doesn't have to be like this!"

No other words from Byron. Tendons popped and ligaments tore and all that could be surgically repaired. All that would heal with time. But something had happened to his heart. How many times had his wife said, "This isn't like you"? How many times did he have to answer that this was who he was now?

One thing's for certain, he wasn't one of *us*—didn't want to be. The word *us* assassinated what was left of his ashamed life. Those paintings were a hulking enemy, utterly unforgivable. Syl was responsible and so was Owen, no matter how nice he'd been. They needed to be held accountable, Byron Settles knew without a doubt. Only one man for a job like that, and so he limped off to tell him.

brutal beautiful treason

There was a small huddle of people waiting outside Damascus's black door. Owen couldn't believe it, as he and Revv stood behind the bar dumbstruck at all the heads waiting to jockey inside for Syl's Olfactory Installation.

The people who comprised this zealous huddle were not the dreary ilk that usually stalked the bar. The hammerheads. The blotto-by-noon. No, these weren't the full-time drinkers who bar-hopped all day, scattering their pathos around the neighborhood—couple drinks here, couple there, on to the next dive—so as to only disfigure their welcome in a particular establishment, never completely defiling it. No, the nine people standing outside of Damascus tonight were preened and young (and employed), all under thirty, it seemed to Owen, who had carded so many customers over the years he had an uncanny knack for knowing people's ages.

"Welcome," he said as he opened the bar for business. He should've been excited—he'd wanted some new life in the place for years now—but his mind was on Byron. Sure, Owen had only known him a handful of days, but they'd really bonded. Or Owen had really bonded. It went to hell so fast. What did it say about Owen's barren life—the rate with which he'd suctioned to a kindred lush?

"Where's your sleigh parked?" one of the eager, preened customers said, laughing at his own joke. Faint smirks from his squirming colleagues. "I knew we took a wrong turn," he said and laughed harder.

Owen sighed; he'd get used to the Santa gags. Hell, if he'd tolerated birthmark cracks his whole life, then Christmas quips should be easy. "Are you all here for the art opening?"

They nodded, and the comedian said, "Do you have shorter barstools so your elves can get sloshed?" really cracking up this time, wiping a pleased tear from his eye.

"No offense, boss," Revv said once Owen came back around the bar again; both men were working this shift together, an arrangement neither necessarily enjoyed, but certain busy nights called for four arms slinging drinks. "I don't understand why all these people are swarming your fine, fine establishment," he said to Owen.

"Must be your charming service."

"Or your Santa suit. Man, I'm hungover," Revv said. "I got a new tattoo last night."

"You worked last night."

"After work."

"Someone tattooed you at two in the morning?"

"Someone tattooed me at five in the morning." Revv rolled up the sleeve on his shirt, and there it was, *sick with recklessness*, on his scrawny bicep. He had lots of ink and piercings and even had angel wings branded onto his shoulder blades and whenever someone asked him how he was doing, Revv liked to say, "Fuck, fight, or footrace: I'm good to go."

Owen squinted, examining the tattoo, trying to decode the exaggerated script. *Stooges of Frecklespecks? Sloth eats Baltimore? Stuffy socks Barnyard?* He couldn't tell what it said. "Is that English?"

"Yeah, it's English," Revv said. "You have no idea?"

"Nope."

"None?"

"Maybe." Owen getting ready to lie to the kid but then giving up: "Not so much."

"Damnit! I knew Rory was too wasted to tattoo."

"Five in the morning. Jesus, no wonder his hand was shaking."

It's worth noting how excited Revv was to see Syl's show tonight, the dead soldiers and the dead fish. He considered the opening's conceit to be sick with recklessness, too. Admired its danger. He'd gotten to Damascus late in the afternoon to unload the liquor delivery, about an hour removed from Byron's enraged exit. Syl and Daph were hanging the last couple soldiers' portraits (Owen was moping) when Revv walked in, looking like a tousled vampire.

Owen glared at him and released some Byron-induced anger at the kid. "You were supposed to be here half-a-fuckin'-hour ago."

"I have many poor excuses I can give you, boss," Revv said, unfazed by Owen's grumpy slang. "Let me know what kind of mood you're in and I'll select one accordingly."

"Why don't I fire you?"

"Loyalty is a blessing and a curse," Revv mused, "but mostly just a bad business model."

"I can't hear your bullshit right now," Owen said. "Syl needs help putting a CD in the jukebox, would you mind?" and he threw his keys to Revv, who was stoked to oblige this request. In the months he'd worked at Damascus, there hadn't been much of an opportunity for him to hit on Syl: she only came in with Daphne and they always seemed deep in conversation about one thing or another.

Revv caught the keys and waited for Syl to finish fiddling with the final painting. Then she walked toward him and the jukebox. "All ready for your big night?" he said to her.

"God no."

"Why not?"

She thought of Byron Settles, his ire, his misunderstanding of her intention, then tried to banish him from her mind; he was only one witness, one drunken idiotic witness. Who cared what he saw in the portraits? "I'm just anxious, I guess. I really want people to recognize what I'm doing. This isn't just some anti-war thing. It's more than that. It's about the complacent citizens back home."

"You'll do great."

"How do you know?"

He smiled at her and unlocked the jukebox. "Because I'm sure you've worked hard getting ready for all this."

"I guess."

"Then there's nothing to worry about. The show is just like practicing, except people are watching."

"That's not like practicing at all," Syl said.

"Sure it is."

"How do you know?"

"I've played in bands for years. Ever heard of Stink Finger? I used to front them. We had a pretty popular EP. Anyhow, I know all about pre-show jitters. Whatever you do, don't get drunk. Take my word for it. It might seem like a good idea, but next thing you know, you fall off the front of the stage and give yourself a black eye and no one in Stink Finger will talk to you anymore."

"The voice of experience has spoken," she said, trying not to laugh at him. He was oddly charming.

"I still can't believe they fired me," Revv said and loaded the show's soundtrack into the jukebox.

•••••••

People continued to march into Damascus for Syl's show. One was a white guy wearing a Kangol and six gold chains around his neck and a baggy track suit; he listened to an iPod, head bobbing. Owen approached and asked what he'd like, and the guy removed the buds from his ears and said, "You heard that song 'Piss Clean'?"

"Can't say I have."

"It's hip-hop. But universal."

"Uh-okay."

"Track is about a father asking his daughter for some clean

pee before he has to have his urine checked by his parole offi-
cer." And then the guy rapped the next couple of phrases right
in Owen's astonished face:

"Daddy's gotta go/ see his P.O./ so piss clean, baby/ piss clean."

"Sounds like an afterschool special," Owen said.

"For real," the white guy said, adjusting his Kangol. "Wish I'd
thought of that back in the day, yo."

About six o'clock, No Eyebrows came in and sat at the bar,
drank some schnapps, hoping to see Shambles. He'd never seen
so many people in there before. He'd had one of those days
where the pain was worse. He'd thrown up. His equilibrium was
off and he staggered as he walked. One of his metastases was
in his brain and shoved his cerebellum, which regulated balance.

Then Shambles came in with Maya maybe ten minutes later.
They shot a game of pool in the back of the bar. Shambles
didn't say hi to No Eyebrows, didn't know what to say. She had
to apologize for what had happened in the taxi—her part in it.
And if not a whole apology, she needed to explain what had
scared her. Frightened by his sadness and anger, all the things
he'd said, the idea of saving him. She'd refused to go back to
his hotel and once back in her apartment, stayed up all night
thinking about him, wondering what ate his body up more, the
cancer or the rage. Or the guilt over leaving his family. It was as
though he thought the sheer temperature of his lividness might
burn the tumors right out of him. Boil them to pulp. She knew
they had to talk before the night was over, but it would have to
be after the art show, after several glasses of whiskey trussed her
up in armor.

A couple walked up next to No Eyebrows, only one empty
stool left at the bar. He looked at them, thought of his wife,
missed Sally. He started to stand up, legs wobbling: "Please, be
my guest."

The man sat in the empty seat while the woman waited for No Eyebrows to get out of the way. She couldn't believe his face, not a hair on it, looked ridged, like a beehive. That sickly color. The circles under his eyes, she'd never seen a face so... well, infested. It was right there, death; it peered at her, offered its chair. "On second thought, you sit," she said.

"Please don't take the privilege away from a dying man of offering my chair to a beautiful woman. I insist."

To this, she had no answer.

He stood up, took a wonky step. "Please."

She sat down. "Can we at least buy you a drink?"

"A lass with manners," he said. "That's very generous. Peppermint schnapps, please."

Owen walked over to help the couple, Revv sliding behind him with three draft beers in his hands for other customers.

"Is that you in there, Owen?" the woman said, reaching out and stroking the sleeve of his Santa jacket.

"It sure is, Mired. Daphne will be so glad you two made it. You look gorgeous." She thanked him. Then Owen said to the guy with her, "How are you, Derek? What can I get you to drink?"

"Coupla Buds."

No Eyebrows, still in the vicinity, awaiting his complimentary schnapps, wondered why Owen never asked how he was holding up. Was it too futile for people to even inquire? The woman looked at him, nudged her boyfriend, and reminded him to buy No Eyebrows' drink. Derek called the addition down to Owen, who nodded, then brought the round to them in about thirty seconds.

They all had their drinks. "Cheers," she said, and No Eyebrows thanked her and she smiled at him, one of her front teeth crooked, like Sally's, and her eyes that same deep green, the color of cucumber peel. Still smiling, that beautiful crooked tooth and No Eyebrows said, "Cheers," drinking his whole shot, hoping it would help his shaking hand, which jiggled as if he played an invisible tambourine.

A disheveled man-boy called to Owen, "Mommy's milk! I need a glass of mommy's milk, stat!"

"Hold your horses, Rhonda," Owen said to him. He was one of the semi-regulars that Owen could have done without. Bad enough he acted like a drunken toddler, did somebody really have to give him a girl's name? Shouldn't there be an emasculation-throttle?

"My horses need a sippy-cup of mommy's milk."

"Don't do this stunted-child thing."

"But I am a stunted child. Everybody knows that."

Down the bar, Daphne gave Owen a predetermined signal, and he finished getting Rhonda's "sippy cup of mother's milk" (whiskey) and then Owen turned the jukebox's volume off.

"May I have everyone's attention," Daphne said.

There were still people talking.

"Attention, please!" she yelled.

People quieted down.

"Welcome," Daphne said, "my name is Sister Truth Serum." Which was her stage name, or one of them—also known to locals as Sister T and sometimes just Truth, the last being the nickname that inflamed Syl's artistic jealousy; it was awful to walk into a bar with Daphne and have someone say, "The Truth is here!" and then buy Daphne a drink, barely acknowledging Syl's presence. Daph was entrenched in the indie art scene. She'd published three poetry collections that had sold decently and had performed across the country in slam festivals, gaining a following for the natural hostility she exuded, the knack to pick the right rhythm of syllables to make an entire audience gasp, truly gasp in amazement.

She continued her introduction to the crowd: "This is the world premiere of *Did You Know These Soldiers Died for You?* by one of my favorite local artists, Sylvia Suture, who graciously asked if I'd open the show with a new poem. Thanks again for being here. Tonight is all about truth. There's going to be so much truth tonight that you'll all go home and refuse to pay your federal taxes until there's an explanation for America's latest war, the regularly scheduled exercise in never minding our own business."

Clapping.

Someone called out, "Tell it to us, Sister Truth."

Another: "Slay 'em, Truth!"

Daph closed her eyes. "This poem's called 'Our Empire.'" She took a few deep breaths, and spoke at a deliberately slow pace at first that built in velocity as she neared the poem's conclusion:

Prison guards in garter belts
tie their tongues
in knots
at our hives of torture.
Silent treatment,
so loud with hoarse throats begging,
pummeled with patriotic fists.
These forked and bloated tongues,
slick with disease
and gluttony
and murder,
slowly waggling.
Our cancerous empire keels,
coughs,
death rattles and dirt raining like confetti
onto our pillaged souls.

More applause, louder.

People yelling and whistling.

A woman said, "Truth Serum is my favorite cocktail."

"Sister, preach!" added another.

Revv whistled.

Daphne thanked everyone, hushed the room, and said, "Now, for the evening's main attraction. It's my esteemed pleasure to introduce Sylvia Suture," and Daphne disappeared to the periphery. The lights dimmed. Syl had been waiting right out front of Damascus, listening to Daph's poem, and now, clad in full camouflage, including camo face paint and combat boots, Syl walked in carrying a big bucket of water with twelve live catfish in it. She wore a tool belt, a hammer on her hip, nails in a leather compartment. She walked to the middle of the room, the middle of the crowd, and plopped the bucket down, spilling water on the floor. People did their best to give her room.

She walked over to the jukebox, put a dollar in, selected the CD she and Revv had loaded earlier that day; Owen turned the volume up again, and seconds later, the beating sound of helicopter blades pulsed over the bar's speakers. Syl moved back into the center of the room. She pulled a glove from her tool belt, a glove that had its palm studded with pieces of sticky rubber, which made it easier to grip fish. While she'd practiced these murders in her living room, she discovered these gloves were necessary to hold the writhing creatures. Yes, she had practiced the killings: if the death sequences at the opening were going to represent such a supreme component of the Olfactory Installation (symbolic sacrifice), then she couldn't leave anything to chance. There had to be a mastering of these murder sequences. No margin for error, even if that meant some members of the animal kingdom were offered up to the gods in dress rehearsals before the martyrs died in actual pageantry.

She slid the studded glove on and said, "Tonight, we're here to talk about a bird with an injured left wing that's been flying in tiny right circles since January 20th, 2001, the day George W. Bush took office."

Syl leaned down and snatched a live catfish from the bucket.

Held it up high over her head. It flopped and bucked. Some people in the audience gasped. Revv cheered. Mutters from the corners. Concern. Shock. She said, "I'd love to tell you that no animals were harmed in the making of our history, but I can't do that. We send soldiers off to die. Usually for no good reason. And this fish will die. It will die, not in vain, but to help us all remember something: people perish every day in the Middle East. Our men and women, our soldiers, are murdered every day." The fish flopped in her hand. "And don't lose sight of the only important fact about Iraq: we were lied to. Our president told us that Saddam Hussein had Weapons of Mass Destruction and if we didn't invade, the madman would blow up everything. Only a different madman is currently succeeding, Our Madman, all in the name of oil." She walked from the center of the room to one of her portraits and used the fish to point at it. "Forget your voting history, your party affiliation. This is Chase Anthony Turgets. He was from Hart, Michigan. He was killed on urban patrol in Fallujah. He died because the president lied to all of us."

She looked around the room. They all waited to see what she was going to do next. Revv hoped for the chance to establish eye contact with her, but her eyes grazed the crowd too quickly.

"I'm going to need a volunteer from the audience to help me," Syl said.

No one volunteered. Revv started to put his hand up, but Owen waved it down, made a face to say: *don't forget that you're working, dumb ass.* Daphne was going to count to ten and if no one stepped up, she'd help Syl, though she hoped that since people had already heard her perform that there would be new blood willing to get up and participate.

Finally (and surprising himself) No Eyebrows called out, "I'd be happy to help," and Syl, like a hammy magician, asked the crowd to give him a nice round of applause for his courage, which they did.

He walked to her. She thanked him. Helicopter blades still

beating. With her free hand she gave him a nail and Syl stuck the catfish flush against the canvas, next to Chase Anthony Turgets' face. She removed the hammer from the holster and said, "Please put the nail to the fish's head." Revv could have kissed her, loved her scandalous patriotism. No Eyebrows, a devout Democrat, loved it, too. He held the nail to the fish's head, watched its mouth pucker as its body thrashed.

"He died because the president lied to all of us," Syl said again, nailing the catfish to the plywood-canvas. No Eyebrows let go. They both stood there, watching its agony. Everyone wide eyed. Cameras flashed.

"Why did he die?" she asked the audience.

"He died because the president lied to all of us!" they shouted.

Fallout from the nailing of the fish spread through everyone, having private deliberations within themselves because they couldn't discuss it out loud yet, couldn't decompress what they'd just witnessed. Not until the show was over. Owen's immediate reaction was selfish, simply, *what have I done, what have I agreed to?* As soon as she nailed the fish—it seized wildly on the plywood—he imagined his bar completely empty for the next thirty days, stinking of rotting corpses.

Shambles wasn't even thinking about the fish. She watched No Eyebrows. Watched him and was fascinated by him. Watched him and wondered where this unwavering powerful kinetic urge had come from inside of her. She couldn't get him out of her mind, and she didn't know why.

Most people observing the nailing of the fish felt pride. Pride in Syl's convictions. Pride that somebody was willing to do something so unacceptable. Her audacity created support from the audience.

To be fair, there was a smattering of people who registered Syl's slaying of the fish as gratuitously offensive. These people would leave Damascus tonight and never come back; they'd tell appalled friends about an indie artist who'd "masturbated all over the place." And there were a few who were outright incensed over the nailing. It was disgusting to waste life like that. One woman left and immediately contacted PETA. Animal rights had always been near and dear to her, and this carnage was just as cataclysmic as dog fighting or dolphins dying in tuna nets. One thing she knew about PETA—they'd act swiftly. She could envision hundreds of protesters at Damascus by early next week.

Revv thought he was in love with Syl. Seriously. That he'd fallen in love because of every word and action she'd performed. This was the kind of brutal beautiful treason that mesmerized him, controlled him; this was the work of an iconoclast, which was a word he didn't toss around. It meant something to him. Pure subversion.

"We'll never forget you, Chase Turgets," someone called out.

People clapped.

More camera flashes.

Revv couldn't stop himself from yelling out: "Chase died so Bush's daughters could go to Ivy League schools and pay $4.00 a gallon for gas!"

Owen scowled at him.

Another person made a noise like a car starting up.

More clapping and camera flashes.

Helicopter blades still beating.

Someone said, "We'll remember your sacrifice, Chase."

Syl looked around at everyone. Frozen and staring at her. She had them eating out of her hand. This was what she'd dreamed of. This was high-wire performance. "I need another volunteer from the audience," she said and this time, almost everyone sent a hand up in the air.

"Let me remind you of something," Syl said. "This isn't the art show. The show hasn't started yet. You all are a part of its genesis. The show starts once the fish begin to decompose. It starts once this room stinks so much of death that you can't think of anything else except mortality. There's nothing in your mind but the fact that the twelve people hanging here all died because of that one single lie. All these massacres in the name of oil. You," Syl said, and pointed at a young woman, "you're next." Then: "And how about another big round of applause for our first brave volunteer."

No Eyebrows waved and walked back to the bar, smiling, thinking of his daughter, of fading from her memory. Hoping that she'd forget the way he'd been since his diagnosis. It wasn't his fault, he wanted to tell her. I'm a hostage in this body and I'm sorry and I wish there was some way for you to know that I love you, some way that you could know what I was like before all this. Some way you could hear me sing, or I could have cooked your favorite meal, or walked you down the aisle to give you away to a worthy husband. But no: there's no chance of that: I'm doomed to give you away in another manner entirely. And I'm sorry.

Syl and her new volunteer walked to the next portrait. This one of Jessica Kathryn Ullestad, who had died, Syl informed the audience, in a suicide bombing three miles outside of Baghdad.

"And why did she die?" Syl baited them on.

In an eager chorus: "She died because the president lied to all of us!" and the volunteer held the nail to its head and Syl brought the hammer down, crushing the fish against the plywood.

"Not everyone counts casualties on high-def TVs," Syl shouted and thought of Byron Settles—would he understand the paintings more if he heard her talk like this? "Some of us care more than that."

More cheering.

And more volunteers were chosen and more catfish were nailed to the canvases and there were more hollers from the crowd and more flashes from cameras and helicopter blades beating and Syl was so happy. As the last fish was fixed to the final portrait—this one of Hector Valente Escolante—Syl looked at all of the paintings and saw that in a moment of morbid ser-endipity, none of the fish had died yet. All twelve fish squirmed on the canvases. Flopping. Waving their bodies at the audience. Saluting.

smart fuckers

There were other things happening in the world, of course. A woman scuba diving off of Cozumel was spooked by the size of a wolf eel and ascended to the surface too quickly and spent eight hours in a hyperbaric chamber to steady her oxygen levels. No Eyebrows' wife, Sally, was making up another lie to tell their daughter—"Your daddy needs more tests, sweetie. But he loves and misses you very much. He wanted me to tell you that." Three more American soldiers were killed in Iraq; five in Afghanistan. There were severe floods in the Tabasco and Chiapas regions of Mexico, killing about 3,000, though that was a conservative estimate. Iran reiterated that it was cultivating a nuclear program solely for energy production. In San Francisco, in North Beach, Sam, the Gulf War vet we've been spying on, was being told about Damascus's art show that evening, and he couldn't believe his ears, temper flooding with bile and a bit of joy, and he said to Byron Settles, "Where exactly is this place?"

Byron had met Sam about six weeks back, on another of his spontaneous, accidental drinking tours to San Francisco (who wanted to stay in Sacramento when the city was only an hour away?). He was in a burger shop, waiting on a double-double, and saw a dog tag tattooed on Sam's neck, across his Adam's apple. They sat next to each other at the shop's cafeteria-style counter. Most of the normal info had been omitted from the tattoo—last name, first and middle initials, Social Security number, blood type, gas mask size, religious preference.

It had only this: USMC.

"I got that stupid Devil Dog after boot camp," Byron said by way of a salutation. "A bunch of us did. Now I've got a cartoon bulldog on my chest, and every time I see it, all I can think is Jesus, man, a bulldog, a damn bulldog, that's the best we could come up with?"

"Shit, my grandpa has that one."

"Rub it in, motherfucker."

"Oo-ra," said Sam, "lemme buy you a cold one."

And a couple fellow marines shoveling burgers get telling each other stories pretty fast—I did this and you should have seen that and I didn't expect to be in the middle of it but there we were, and to tell the truth Byron wasn't telling much truth— how could he?—didn't mention his two-second war, outlining instead what he knew had happened that day at Bashur. Turned out Sam was a Medical Discharge himself, newly home, blind in his dominant eye after taking a gnat-sized piece of shrapnel in it, metal from a car's bumper. The iris's coloring was no longer solid brown, but had a milky lattice underneath the pupil. Always incredibly bloodshot. The metal was still wedged behind his eye, tiny culprit back by the optic nerve, too risky for the doctors to remove.

Byron knew right where to find Sam after leaving Damascus flaming pissed that afternoon. In fact, Sam had straight up told Byron, "This bar stool is my post now. And I take it very serious." So Byron cabbed over to the Irish pub (what is it with marines and Irish bars?) and they started throwing 'em back, annoyed about Syl's portraits at first but just shaking their heads, commiserating, civilians, artists, ridiculous but what can you do, why are we defending them anyway? Their reactions got stronger, meaner, as the late afternoon meandered into evening which flowered into night, and now Sam wanted to see Damascus, take in these disgusting pictures for himself, talk to the proprietor— point at his dead eye and say, "I lost this for you and this is how you treat us? This is how you pay back all the soldiers, sailors, and marines who gave the greatest sacrifice?"

"We can go tell him to take them down," Byron said.

"Or we can fuck him up."

"Let's just scare him."

"Or we fuck him up," Sam again advocated.

Meanwhile, across town, in Damascus, Owen closed the bar after the Olfactory Installation; everyone had left except Syl and Daph and Revv, the three of them sitting at the bar drinking whiskey while Owen tried hopelessly to count all the money in the till.

"I can't keep it straight," he said. "The total keeps changing."

"Did Christmas come early for Santa?" Daphne asked.

He smiled. "This is more than I've ever made in one night. I think, anyway. Jesus, I'm so drunk that counting is killing me." Then Owen looked over at Syl and said, "My thanks, my dear."

"Thank you for hosting the show in the first place. Plenty of places passed on the chance."

"Better for us," he said.

They drank another shot of whiskey and Owen spilled down the front of his Santa jacket (yet another garnish on it). Everyone laughed. He wasn't alone in his nearing blackout: they all had a sturdy heat on.

"So," Daphne said to Syl, "what did you think of your big night?"

"That was the best night of my life. I've never felt so... so much like a conduit. I think that people were into it."

"What's sixty plus forty-seven?" Owen asked them.

"107."

"107? That can't be right." He shook his head and started over.

"Everyone was riveted," Daphne said to Syl. "You could have heard a pin drop."

"Over the helicopters?" Revv said.

"Shhh," Daph said. "I'm proving a point."

"And I agree with you," he said. "The show was bitchin'. You should be really proud, Syl. I'm gonna grab another beer. You girls want one?"

"Whatever you're having is fine."

"You sure? I proudly drink the crappiest beer in America: Miller High Life."

"Why?" they said.

"High Life for a lowlife," he said. "Sounds like a Bukowski poem, don't it?"

They asked for draft pilsners instead of High Lifes.

"Now I have to wait for the reviews," Syl said.

"Screw the critics," Revv said, pushing the beers across the bar to them, then coming back around and planting himself. "You made real deal art so don't worry whether any academic dimwits get it or not. Let them snicker at cartoons in *The New Yorker*. The joke's on them. Intellectuals aren't artists because they don't want dirt under their manicures. And I'm not just talking about the women."

"I agree—who cares what they say?" Daph said.

"Revv, get your ass over here and help me count," Owen barked.

"I'll do it," Daphne said, winking at Syl, leaving her and Revv alone to chat. "Nothing sadder than my liquored-up uncle Santa Claus struggling with arithmetic."

"I'm really impressed," Revv whispered to Syl once Daph was out of earshot. "Your show'll get the stooges thinking during the commercial breaks. Where did you get the idea to kill the fish?"

She hadn't really talked with anyone about this. She'd been a bit apprehensive to disclose too much about it, figuring people would frown on her sitting around her apartment and slaughtering life. "I knew I wanted to kill something and they were easy to get. Plus, I hoped they'd look badass squirming on the canvasses."

"They did. Me and you have something in common," Revv said. He rolled the sleeve on his shirt up and pointed at his *sick with recklessness* tattoo: "That's the story of our lives."

Syl squinted at it. "What does it say?"

"You can't read it, either?"

"Nope."

"Damnit, Rory. I'm gonna kill you."

"Who's Rory?"

"A soon-to-be formerly alive tattoo artist."

"Sorry."

"It says *sick with recklessness*. After I saw you perform tonight, I knew you had the same disease as me."

"What disease?"

"We don't want any more hypocrisy. We're sending it back." Then, out of nowhere, Revv said something that Syl agreed with so thoroughly she wanted to lean over and kiss him. "Art should stir shit," he said.

"Totally."

"Once it does, then people can stake their side. Art should be an accusation. That's what it's all about."

Then she did kiss him. "I like your ideas," she said afterward.

"Of course you do: I'm right."

"And insecure."

"Do you know who you look like?" he said, turning on his rough and tumble charm.

She bristled. "Don't say Harry Potter."

"Why would I say Harry Potter?"

"Never mind."

"You really couldn't read my tattoo?"

Syl shook her head. "Sorry."

"Do you wanna come have a drink at my place?"

"Sure," she said, because she figured why not. He was cute

and tatted to the gills and he'd just said, "Art should stir shit," and Syl loved that idea, the urban *patois* with which he expressed it, loved thinking of herself as *the conduit*, a trigger. Sex sounded like the perfect ending to the best night of her artistic life, the highest her wire had ever been (so far). Plus, he was a decent kisser. Or close enough to decent. And if Syl was hell-bent on getting laid, he was the only man in the room who wasn't wearing a Santa suit.

"I hope you like Jäger," Revv said. "It's all I have around the *casa*."

"Let's steal a bottle of wine from Owen."

"I try not to steal that much stuff from here anymore."

"I was kidding," Syl said.

"Oh. Yeah. Of course. Me, too."

"May we procure a bottle of red wine, please, Owen?" Syl asked him.

"Huh?" He hadn't heard the beginning of what she said, just his name, still trying to count the ten dollar bills. (The bank would later tell him that he was still a few bucks off.) "What did you say, Syl?"

"Can Revv and I borrow a bottle of wine? We're going back to his place."

Daph shot Syl a face of feigned surprise. "Oh, are you..."

"Oh, I are," Syl said. "Call you in the morning, Mother Dearest."

"Take whatever booze you want," Owen said. "Revv normally just yanks shit and thinks I don't notice."

"I don't just yank shit."

"You do."

"I don't."

"Then we should call an exterminator. Because we obviously have mice that can haul entire bottles of Jäger."

••••••••

Twenty minutes down the road, Revv and Syl were long gone,

and Owen walked his niece outside, kissed her on the forehead. "I know we're the only family we got left," he said, "but I wouldn't trade you in for anybody. You're growing into an amazing woman."

"Thanks."

"Your ma would've loved your poem tonight, Daphne."

"You think?"

"If you're this remarkable in your late twenties, what are you going to be capable of in your thirties?" he asked her. "I can't wait to watch."

"I don't think like that. Try and help some kids read. Write new poems of my own. Help my uncle."

"How did William's essay turn out: 'Baristas of the real world'?"

"Not bad," Daphne said, because she didn't want to get into it. Truth was that William refused to budge. He was convinced he knew better and she'd stopped pushing, fine with her, it was your future, and she'd like fries and a large Coke to go with her burger, thanks, William. But it bothered Daph. Especially when the kid had asked, "Are you sure you know what you're doing?" Of course, she did.

"You're a good teacher," Owen said to her.

"I'm thinking about getting my credential and teaching high school English in the city."

"You have something I never had. You have promise. And I get the privilege of seeing all your accomplishments."

"You're really drunk," she said. "Is this going to be one of those sleeping bag/pool table nights?"

"Don't ask, don't tell, baby." He thought of Byron, his midnight confidante, sprawled out and yammering back and forth. Then he thought of Byron's balled fists and how weird it was watching him stomp away.

"Would you rather crash at my place?" Daph asked.

"I'm fine here."

"Are you sure?"

"It's worked for me so far."

"I'm not sure that's true."

"Either way…"

"I'll come by in the morning to check on you," Daph said. "Any breakfast requests?"

"Surprise me."

"Goat balls?"

"Don't surprise me that much. Think hangover-food."

"Something greasy?"

"I wouldn't complain about grease, no."

"I love you," she said, making her way down the sidewalk. "You're my favorite 'barista of the real world.'"

Hearing that, his day was officially made. "Love you, too."

Then he went back to collect all the empty bottles from behind the bar; he would set them on the sidewalk for the homeless to recycle. Their currency. He considered it his contribution to the neighborhood economy; he hadn't given spare change, not one nickel, to a homeless person in over twenty years.

His mind moved away from Byron and Daph. He thought only of Damascus, which made him beam a bit: the bar had been jammed, everyone seemed to enjoy themselves, and he'd done something good, supporting the local art scene (even if a certain absent bagel dog didn't agree). He'd been rewarded with a cash register containing almost $1800.

There were so many spirit bottles that it was going to take him a few trips to dispose of them all, loading them into cardboard boxes and lugging them out front. He propped the door open to make the work easier, not that it really felt like work. In a blissful high. He wore the Santa suit—a new liquor stain on its graying trim—which meant Hitler had vacated his face, and now, like a delicious cherry on top, the bar's business boomed all night.

He walked out front, set a box of bottles down.

"Hey," a man said, walking toward him from across the street.

Owen couldn't tell who it was but figured it was another homeless guy trying to monopolize the night's bottles; it was a competitive industry to secure a bar's whole take, wouldn't be long before other prospectors showed up to try and stake their clanking claims.

"Good timing," Owen said. "There are more boxes inside. Help me grab them and they're yours."

The man didn't say anything.

Owen turned around and walked back into Damascus.

The man followed behind him.

The man shut the front door.

Drunk, Owen hadn't noticed what the man had done. Instead, he moved behind the bar, picked up a box, and extended it in the man's direction. Trying to be friendly, Owen said, "Make sure to lift with your legs, not your back."

The man didn't move.

"All yours," Owen said affably.

"What is?"

"The bottles."

"You can keep your bottles, Santa Claus."

"Huh?"

"I'm not here for those."

"Why are you here?" Owen looked at the man closely for the first time. Was he homeless? Maybe, maybe not. It was hard to tell in San Francisco: gutter punks and dot com millionaires often shopped in the same secondhand stores. His hair was cropped short. Dirty blond. A long goatee hung from his chin like cheese falling from a slice of pizza. A dog tag tattooed across his Adam's apple. Black jeans and a torn button-down shirt with grease or oil stains on it.

"I'm here about your artwork."

"Were you at the opening?"

"I wasn't," the man said. "You'd have known if I'd been

here. I'd have been the motherfucker who slapped that cunt across the face and told her to shut her despicable fucking mouth."

"I'll call the cops," Owen said and set the box of empty bottles back down on the floor.

"You aren't going to call nobody. But I am." He pulled out his cell and seconds later said into the phone, "Come on in. Santa seems more nice than naughty this evening."

"You can have all the money," Owen said.

"Let's wait for our mutual acquaintance. He should be here in no time." And in no time, Byron Settles pushed Damascus's door open, then locked it behind him.

"What's going on?" Owen said to Byron, who made sure not to look at him, saying only, "You should've listened to me."

"Don't worry about Byron right now," the man said to Owen. "Worry about me. My name's Sam. It's best if you don't make me mad. I can be a little"—Sam held his hand out, fingers extended, and wobbled it back and forth—"unstable. I've got one of those 4th of July tempers: explosions galore lighting up the sky."

Owen didn't say anything, watched a sick smile toil its way onto Sam's face. Then Sam sat down at the bar and said, "I know it's after last call, but would you be willing to bend the rules for a couple good Americans? I'd like a shot of Bacardi 151; as you know, Byron is partial to Hennessy."

"You can have whatever you want." Owen poured the drinks and set them in front of the men. He tried to catch Byron's eyes. No luck.

"That's what I like about you, Santa," Sam said. "You're a bartender who's willing to tinker with the rules for a worthy customer." He drank it and asked for another. Owen poured, left it sitting in front of him. "Now what's this I hear about paintings that disrespect soldiers?"

"It was an art opening," Byron said, and Sam answered

quickly, angrily, "Santa and I are talking right now, B. Why don't you drink your Hennessy and be quiet for a bit, all right?"

Byron nodded, sipped his shot. The way he figured it, he was either letting down Owen or he was betraying everybody in his unit, the whole Corps. It wasn't much of a contest, or so he pretended. All that was going to happen was he and Sam would intimidate Owen into taking the portraits down. No real harm done. Owen needed to know that certain things were not up for debate—you couldn't use soldiers as artwork. People weren't trophies.

"Thing is," Sam said, "I get all ornery when I hear about things that upset me, and unfortunately for you, this shit upsets me a lot." He drank his 151 and asked for another. Owen refilled his glass. "Is this the art?" Sam looked around the room.

Owen nodded and said, "I'm sorry."

"You will be," said Sam, slipping into a role he missed, one he coveted. He felt locked away in a "Sane Asylum" since being home. Everything here so sensible. So timid and tidy and polite. There's an arhythmia to war. Music without a time signature. And yes, there's an excitement, too: you're trained to kill and you want to kill, you want the glory, the bloodshed. Living like that—day in, day out—plugged into that kind of high wire act, well, Sam mourned it. He classified himself as M.I.I. since being back, *Missing In Inaction*.

Byron sat at the bar, taking tiny sips of Hennessy. Not looking at Owen or Sam, only staring down at his drink, falling, still falling… Sam would put the fear of god in Owen, and they'd be out the door in five minutes.

There was the issue of the baseball bat, which Owen kept behind the bar in case he needed to deter any drunkards from smashing up Damascus. Picking it up right now, however, seemed like a bad idea. Owen was so loaded he couldn't have hit a refrigerator with it. Even if he wasn't exorbitantly drunk—let's not tell tales out of school—he wouldn't have picked the bat up anyway. He was outnumbered and the way Byron deferred to Sam scared Owen. So he stood there idiotically. Sweating. Panicking. Short of breath. Trying not to cry. He took off his Santa hat and set it on the bar, scratched his head.

Sam walked around Damascus, looking at each of the soldiers' portraits. One hand in his pocket, the other holding his drink. Relaxed. Perusing. "What kind of art is this?"

"They're portraits of dead soldiers," Owen said.

Sam stuck a finger out and touched one of the dead fish. "And what are these unfortunate creatures for?"

"The artist wanted to make sure the pictures smelled like war."

"Smells like bullshit," Byron said, still staring at his Hennessy glass, which was now empty.

Owen wanted to tap him on the shoulder, to remind him of the pillow-talk they'd shared. Wanted to say, okay, we don't agree about these paintings, but we're friends, don't do this, Byron, please don't let this man hurt me…

"I think what Byron means is that you should stick to what you know. Wrap presents and feed your reindeer and screw Mrs. Claus. You don't know anything about war so shut your mouth about that."

"Do you want the money?"

"I want an eyeball," said Sam.

"Wait, what?" Byron asked, knowing there was no way Owen could defend himself if Sam got physical. Maybe nothing Byron could do about it either. He remembered something from his first few days of basic training, a sergeant asking one of the weaker guys to do ten push-ups. That was all he had to do: ten straight push-ups. Everybody was lined up watching. The guy got down and did the first one, and as his arms straightened back out getting ready for the second, the sergeant kicked him square in the ribs. He fell over. The sergeant said every time he fell, he'd start from the beginning. The guy tried another. Kick.

Fall. Start over. He never got past two. It was awful standing and watching, nothing you could do about it. Byron saw the guy with his shirt off a couple days later, ribs black as seal blubber.

"Let me handle this, B," Sam now said.

"We should take the paintings and get out of here," Byron said. "Give them a proper burial."

"In due time." Sam still peered at the pictures, but now he turned around and glowered hard at Owen. The Sane Asylum crumbling around him, a welcome rage barreling through him, hypersonic, piercing; Sam could feel hunks of danger in his blood, like pulp in juice. "Soldiers aren't fish. Byron and me won't let you piss all over them."

Nothing from Owen.

"So about that eyeball," Sam said and took another sip of his 151.

"We're giving you one chance to take the paintings down," Byron blurted. "Take them down before you open the bar tomorrow."

"Why should he get a warning?" Sam asked.

"I told you he took me in for a couple nights. That earns him a warning, man. Come on."

"Does it?"

"It does."

Sam didn't answer, standing enamored in front of one particular portrait. With his fingernail, he scratched at one of the portrait's eyes, kept digging at it until the paint was gone and you could see the plywood underneath where the eye had been. He looked at the paint wedged under his fingernail, picked it out with his teeth and spit it on the floor. "I lost an eye protecting you," Sam said to Owen. "Only seems right for you to give me one of yours."

"Take 'em down. This is your only warning," Byron said.

"I don't give warnings," Sam said. "Thank your lucky stars Byron's here."

Byron Settles looked up at Owen's sky and thought of their camping trips, shooting stars. "Don't call the cops. Don't be a hero. Take 'em down and everything's fine."

Owen nodded.

Sam said, "You named this place Damascus, but I don't think that's the right name for it. You all seem to know so much, maybe you should change the name." He paused, then snapped his fingers. "You should call it Smart Fuckers. You are all so smart, that's the only name that will do this place justice."

"This ain't my fault," Byron said to Owen. "I told you not to let her hang this. It's on you, man, not me."

"My fault," Owen said.

The last words out of Sam's mouth, speaking back at a normal volume, were, "Does it seem like I'm fucking around?" and Owen shook his head, saying, "No, sir," and Sam said, "I'll get my eye," and Sam smiled, he and Byron leaving Damascus. Owen ran over and locked the door and slid to the ground and looked up at his man-made stars and clouds, hyperventilating.

Part Two

(Costco… tie your camels… our idiotic epiphanies… a guy goes into another bar… mastectomy scars… right hand of the law… erotic sedition… the hazy illusion of healing… *the reason!*… recycling man…)

real life

No Eyebrows knew that he needed to leave his family once and for all after a trip to, of all absurd places, Costco. That dizzying mega-store, your one-stop-shop to purchase a CD player and salmon filets and a pair of jean shorts and a paper shredder. Costco sold things in devastating supplies, vast quantities of merchandise reassuring every customer that they would live forever.

3,000 tablets of Pepto Bismol.

500 frozen lamb shanks.

10 gallons of salsa.

3 pounds of cumin.

This particular day, No Eyebrows was a little less than a week removed from a chemo treatment. Carboplatin and Paclitaxel. A rugged combination of orange liquid wormed into the portacath mounted in his shoulder; the portacath now a necessity because his veins were shrunken and useless; the juice trickled into him for six hours, and he wished he possessed the ability for a positive outlook. But he didn't. This was stage-four lung cancer. Stage-four of four. No survivors. No chance. No hope. No contingency plan. No *deus ex machina*. No last ditch effort. No negotiations. No eyebrows.

Things were so futile in fact that his oncologist had said to him, "All you can do now is tie your camels and leave the rest to god."

"Tie my camels?"

"It's an old Sufi adage. Tie your camels, in this case, means doing your treatments, taking care of the part of this process that's within your control. But with stage-four, faith is a big part of this. Whatever, whoever you believe in, it'll be a part of your healing process."

"What if I don't believe in god?"

"Are you sure you don't?" the doctor asked.

"I'm sure."

"You haven't become more curious about an afterlife since your diagnosis?"

"That happens?"

"Regularly."

"I don't think I can start believing in something simply because I'm dying."

The oncologist pondered this for a moment: "Then you just tie your camels, I guess. Just tie them and hope." The doc smiled. "You do believe in hope?"

"I'm so mad this is happening to me."

"There's nothing wrong with believing," the oncologist said. "Belief can keep us alive for a long time."

No Eyebrows had already outlived their estimates on expectancy, although this fact didn't make him feel any better. Really, it confirmed his suspicion that none of the "experts" really knew what they were talking about. They could tell you what was killing you but couldn't do anything to stop it. An MRI or CAT or PET scan, No Eyebrows had come to believe, were curses, like clairvoyance: the savvy to see the future but without the talent to alter it. All that was left for No Eyebrows was the forgotten art of camel tying.

Typically, for the week or so following a chemo treatment, he could do nothing but lie in bed, nauseated and freezing and head pounding and more tired than he'd ever been. The numbing in his feet heightened during these stretches; it was what made driving so difficult, never knowing how hard his foot pressed the pedals, if they pressed the pedals at all. A burning in his stomach. He oscillated between days of constipation and then gruesome diarrhea. And, oddly, as his oncologist was surprised at this particular side effect, his hearing would decrease after each treatment, slowly returning to normal.

He was nearing the end of this round of chemo (every three weeks for seven months). Sally now had to give him daily Neupogen injections to up his white cell count. He was beyond exhausted and despite Sally's requests that he relax and recuperate—*I'm only going to Costco, for god's sake*—he insisted on coming along.

"We used to always go together," he reminded her, "and split a hotdog as we walked out. Remember?"

Yes, she remembered. She remembered everything that had once seemed simple, prosaic, but was now impossible. Like laughing. Vacation. Dinner parties. Walks on the bike trail. Martinis. Sex.

"Are you sure you're up to it?" she said.

He nodded and bundled up, wearing a sweater underneath a pea coat. A beanie for his bald head. Two pairs of socks on his dead feet.

She drove and he said, "Let's listen to some music."

"You're feeling good?"

"Superb."

She played one of their favorite CDs: Tom Waits's *Real Gone.*

"How's Erica doing?" he said.

"She's scared."

He felt the need to make an impossible statement: "I think I can beat this thing. For the two of you, I think I can do it."

She felt the need to try and ignore his impossible statement: "We need to get gas."

"Do you think I can beat it?"

"I'm really hoping."

They parked, and Sally wheeled the cart, and they entered

Costco, immediately passing the electronics section, laptops and camcorders and televisions longer than caskets. One of the displays was a combination: a camcorder pointing toward the entrance and broadcasting the newly arrived customers on a huge eighty-inch TV.

No Eyebrows saw himself on the screen, bundled up like a refugee, scrawny and pallid; Sally saw them, too, almost winced but caught herself. He could feel his wife stiffen. He said, "Check it out," nudging her and pointing. "We're stars."

She didn't say anything.

He put his arms up like a bodybuilder and pretended to flex. "I'm Mr. Universe, huh?"

"Mr. Universe…" There was that old saying: sometimes all you can do is laugh. Sally didn't believe in that axiom anymore.

"Hollywood, here we come," he said, smiling at her.

She didn't answer.

They walked off screen.

Sally still wasn't saying anything and they turned down an aisle and No Eyebrows said, "Don't feel bad for me. We're shopping together like the old days. Let's have fun, Sally Sue."

"I'm trying."

"I know you are."

"Of course I think you can get better."

"Thanks."

She let go of the cart and they hugged.

"You have to relax," he said, "because you're totally harshing my buzz with your melancholic vibes, man."

She couldn't fight it anymore and laughed. When she got out of her head, when she was able to escape it, this was what she wanted. This was normalcy. It was husband and wife walking side by side, stocking their lives with necessary and unnecessary things. This was real life, or the life they had, or someone else's life. Sally didn't care, merely absorbing every gleaming second of it.

She slowly pushed the cart, and he had the list in his hand. "What's nelgerans?"

"What?"

He pointed. "That's what it says right here."

"Deodorant." She watched his shuddering hand hold the list.

"Are you sure?"

"I'm sure."

"I hope Erica inherits my handwriting. Otherwise, no one will ever know what the hell she's trying to say. How many sticks of nelgerans should I grab? Two, ten, or twenty-five pack?"

"Two is fine, thank you."

He hucked the package into the cart. "I don't know. You never want to run out of nelgerans."

She wheeled on and they bantered and laughed and pitched more items into their cart, and then he slowed, then stopped, saying, "I need a sec."

Sally let go of the cart. "What is it?"

"I need to stand here."

"Are you dizzy?"

"I'm fine."

"What's wrong?"

"Let me steady…"

"Why don't you sit down?"

"Right here?"

"Yes."

"You know I won't do that," he said, but two minutes later he had no choice, plopping down in the aisle. Dizzy. Overheating. Worried he might throw up. An ache deep in his body, his bones.

"Should I call 911?" Sally said.

"I'm fine. But I don't think I can walk anymore."

"Stay here. I'll get some help." Sally quickly walked toward the check-out lines, flagged down an employee. He followed her back to where her husband was sitting. After some deliberation, it was determined that the least offensive option was to get No

Eyebrows in a wheelchair and park him by the food court. Then Sally could quickly complete shopping. They only needed six more things anyway.

The employee wheeled the chair over to No Eyebrows. Sally helped him up and got him sitting in it. The look in his eyes: ferocious humiliation. Everyone who walked by stared.

"I'm sorry," he said.

"Don't be. This gentleman will take you over by the exit. I'll get the last couple things and meet you as fast as I can, okay?"

He nodded.

"Hey," she said, "you didn't do anything wrong."

He nodded again, and the employee wheeled him away.

Sally watched him go and didn't like that this thought went through her mind, but it did: she wished, like the feeling in his feet, that the chemo would numb some of his pride. That he would recognize what everyone else did: he was dying. He had to stop pretending that things were going to get better. He was at the end and she was going to be a widow—*a god damn widow!*— a single mother: she'd never have had a child if she knew this would happen: battling a teenager by herself, fighting a hundred squabbles without her partner's support.

Standing there in Costco. Standing there as he was wheeled away. Standing there surrounded by all these options, everything you could possibly want, prepackaged and waiting for you on one of the aisles. Sally looked at the list and knew the store well enough to walk toward the product located in the closest section. Five minutes, tops; five minutes and she could whisk him away from this agony.

"Would you like some water?" the employee said to No Eyebrows, parking him by the exit.

"Please."

"Be right back."

And he sat there. He could see the TV showing each new customer coming in the front door. He watched for a while. The changing faces. The families. He watched as they flashed on the screen and vanished into the store to stock their lives in bulk.

The employee returned and handed him a Dixie cup of water: "Here you go. My name's Mark. I'll check on you in a few minutes."

"Thanks, Mark." He tried to turn his attention away from the TV. He looked toward the check-out lines but didn't see Sally yet and drank his tiny cup of water and crumpled it in his hand. But he couldn't resist the gravitational pull of his despair and nostalgia and so he looked back at the television, looked at everything he'd miss once his life ended, the men and women and children, people of all ages and sizes and colors, all the healthy, able-bodied people, all their lungs free from tumors, all their stomachs and brains and spines clear of metastases. All of their steady cells. He was supposed to accept it, but he couldn't get past the questions. Why me? Why do I have to die? Why now? Why don't I get to grow old like everyone else?

Meanwhile, Sally snatched the last item on the list, not the last, exactly, but the other three weren't essentials, and she could easily pick them up some other time. Hurrying to check-out.

No Eyebrows peered in another direction. He was sitting adjacent to the food court, though he hadn't really noticed until now, had been too preoccupied with the gigantic TV and all the healthy families trotting across the screen. In the food court, there were five picnic tables and people chomping on snacks. This was the very location he hoped to share a hotdog with his wife, as they walked out from this shopping trip. This was the reason he'd insisted on coming along. It wasn't a show of strength, an indication that he was on the mend faster than normal from his latest treatment. Not at all. It was simply this: five minutes, sitting at a crummy picnic table and passing a hotdog back and forth, like they used to do.

Even if he wasn't able to eat his half, appetite nonexistent, too nauseated; even if Sally had to take one for the team and eat more processed meat and bun and condiments than she'd really wanted to, it would have been something she'd gladly endure. He knew that.

So he sat there, watching a young couple share a piece of pizza.

A mother feed her son French fries doused in ketchup.

An old man (*I want to get old, too, damnit!*) spooning soup to his mouth.

And yes, a hotdog, though it wasn't being passed between him and his wife, one being consumed by a teenager, relish falling off its backend and splattering on the picnic table's checkered cloth.

He sat in a wheelchair, in Costco, and watched all of this.

Sally, luckily, had a knack for picking the fastest check-out lane. Always and without fail. He used to joke, "If only this was a skill we could take to Vegas," and it didn't fail her today, speeding through without a hitch. She ran to him pushing the enormous flatbed cart, observing his doleful gaze, as he stared at the food court. She knew exactly what he was thinking. Synchronicity could be a fickle bitch. "Should we grab a hotdog?" she said. "There's no wait. I'll get one."

"I'm not hungry."

"That's not really the point." She started walking toward the food court.

"Don't."

"For old time's sake?"

Old time's sake, he thought. Why doesn't she just stab me in the heart? "I'm not hungry and I don't feel good. Please."

She walked back over to him.

Mark followed closely behind her: "Can I help you get to the car, sir?"

"Sure, Mark," he said.

She wheeled the cart; Mark wheeled her husband; Sally buckled him in; Mark loaded the groceries; Sally climbed in the driver's seat; Sally started the engine and looked at the gas light and said, "I think we can make it home without getting gas."

"I'll be dead soon," No Eyebrows whispered.

"Don't say that."

"I'm sorry to die on you. I really am."

"Please don't say that."

"I'm sorry," he said and Sally leaned over and hugged him. "I'm sorry things are turning out this way."

"Don't apologize."

"You'll be okay without me. I know you will."

"Kiss me," she said.

And they kissed.

And he said, "I'm going to miss you so much."

And they sat there hugging.

And they sat there crying.

And she said, "I don't know how to raise Erica without you."

And he said, "You're a wonderful mother."

And they sat in the Costco parking lot with the wind blowing and people walking in and out of the store.

And she said, "I love you."

And he said, "I love you."

And they kissed again.

And they cried even harder.

And Sally put the car in reverse.

And she looked at the gas gauge again.

And she reconsidered, saying, "We'll have to stop for gas, after all."

And he reconsidered, too: hadn't she witnessed enough of his ridiculous decline?

stupefying dune of defamation

W ell, if it wasn't bad enough to gut through a week in which Revv had a tattoo engraved on his arm that no one could read—*Sexy time Pandabear? Yankee says Cockblock?*—here he was at the veterinarian's, listening to a technician tell him that the lump in his boa constrictor's belly was Revv's own boxer shorts.

"It ate my undies?"

"Apparently."

"Why would he eat my drawers?"

The tech chuckled. "I don't feel comfortable speaking on your snake's behalf. But I'd assume starvation played some minor role in the mystery."

"Do they eat things like this often?"

"I can safely guarantee you that, no, this does not happen often. He must have been famished."

"I fed him recently."

"When?"

Revv paused at this. When had his boa constrictor—Revv called him his Bowie Constrictor, hoping some day the snake would asphyxiate David Bowie for singlehandedly emasculating rock and roll—last been fed? Two weeks and change, he guessed. It was a solid question. One that might not matter all that much anyway because the fascists wanted $900 to operate and get the boxers out of its digestive tract. Revv loved Bowie, but, come on, $900? That was a lot of scratch to shell out on the snake's behalf. That was his savings, *all of his savings*. If his own parents—that "family" he yanked himself out of at sixteen and never looked back—needed $900 for surgery, he wouldn't give them a dime.

Revv doesn't want you to know the particulars of his past, but you know the story without hearing it: you know about selfish, wanton, ludicrous parents who make their children's lives impossible uphill struggles: you know the biological irony of alcoholism: how kids raised by drunkards go on to be drunkards, even though they hate drunkards...

"Will he definitely die if we let him digest the boxers *au naturel*?" Revv asked.

"Are you kidding me?" the tech said.

"I am not kidding you, dude."

"Yes, he'll definitely die."

"I'm going to need a minute to think it over."

"Think it over? Your pet will die."

"Yeah, but I might die if I give you $900. That's everything I've got."

"We have payment plans."

"Just a sec. I'll need to talk this over with myself."

"Maybe you should check with someone else," the tech suggested.

This wasn't how he planned on spending the morning after getting lucky with Syl. He wanted to lag around his bed and drink coffee and smoke cigarettes with her. Wanted to have another screw. Wanted to hear her talk about the Olfactory Installation because honestly, it had blown his mind; *she* had blown his mind with the beauty in her murders. The shock she splattered on the audience, like heaving chum in their faces, bait to lure the predator right to them. In this case the predator was perspective, a bellowed reminder of the war in Iraq. In fact, all of Revv's heroes from Joe Strummer to Ian MacKaye scolded the populace, laughed at the mainstream, stamped piercing condemnations onto strangers like graffiti on buildings. Someday, Revv would stand on stage and indict, zero in and fire his own caustic and righteous artillery at the stooges. It was his calling. He was sure of it. Now it was just the minor detail of putting a new band together, or joining one already off the ground.

Actually, Syl was the one who had pointed out the snake's weird digestive lump this morning as she sat up on his futon, stretched and wormed her way to its edge, her knees crammed up in her face because the futon was flat on the floor. "What was the last thing you fed it?" she said to him.

"A rat. But that was a couple weeks back."

"It appears to have recently indulged in an ad hoc feast."

"I'm realizing that." Revv's hungover eyes trying to focus on Bowie. "That is not the intended shape of his body. I agree with your assessment."

"Is there a pet equivalent of 9-1-1?"

"Not to my knowledge."

"Because you should probably call somebody soon," Syl said.

"I can take him to a vet, I guess. But I'd rather stay in bed with you."

"It might be dying."

"Hard to say. He's a bit of a diva." Revv pulled her back into bed and kissed her, excited to experience one of his favorite things about new lovers: morning breath. He considered it to be one of the sexiest things you could share with somebody. Hers was like coffee grounds and smoked salmon. He'd written a song about it once, though the chorus wasn't right. It needed to be revised. He'd teach it to the next lot of blokes he jammed with. Maybe it could be the tune to break him out. You didn't need a whole album anymore. Just a solid single. One cut to make the rounds. The internet had changed the music business, even for punk bands. "Let's have one more roll in the hay," he said to Syl.

"But this is how I sneak away," she said, only sort of joking. Getting away early was part of her deal. Better to leave them wanting more than wondering when on earth you were going to come to your estrogen-soaked senses and vacate the premises. Besides, she was still so manically high from the Olfactory Installation, she wanted to call and harass Daphne, get to Damascus early today to see the fishy portraits. "I always feed mysterious objects to guys' pets and skulk off into the distance."

"Are you running away from me?" he asked.

"Not yet. But soon…"

"I want to tell you something serious about the art opening last night," Revv said. "Promise not to laugh at me?"

"Promise." But there was a part of her that was leery of hearing what was coming next.

"I was moved," Revv said.

Instant relief for Syl (irrationally fearing a reference to Harry Potter). She hadn't expected someone like Revv to cop to being moved. And she hadn't expected to *like* hearing it.

He continued: "I know that makes me sound like a douche, but seriously, your art moved me. I've never really had an experience like that before. I felt like I was witnessing something really vital. It's only ever happened to me with rock and roll. You have a real gift. The stuff you're doing can sure stir the shit."

"Thanks. I don't really know what to say."

"Don't say anything," he said.

Syl was taken aback, in a great way. Seeing the world from her high wire. No one had ever pledged that her art had made them feel something. For years that was her sole goal: to elicit an emotional response in a stranger, to make someone she'd never met in person feel something based entirely on the artwork itself.

Her greatest wish was coming true, here in this guy's ludicrously male bedroom, a machine on his dresser that dispensed chilled Jägermeister. He'd shown it off to her last night when they first walked into his room, after introducing her to his eleven—*eleven!*—roommates, rubbing the top of the machine like he was steadying a spooked animal.

"This is my dairy cow, Bessy," he cooed.

Syl was confused. "Nice to meet you, Bessy…"

He poured Jäger shots from Bessy, making motions with his hands like he was milking her. Syl didn't want to belittle his prize possession so she drank the liquor even though she hated the taste.

"Radiant milk, huh?" said Revv. "You can tell she's a happy beast."

"How drunk are you?"

"On a scale of one to ten, I'm pretty shit-faced."

And that was the way life worked, she guessed. These were our idiotic epiphanies. She'd just experienced a monumental moment, one she'd pined for her whole life—hearing how her art had affected someone. Never in a million years did she imagine receiving this news while planted on a mashed futon a few feet away from a Jäger machine named Bessy. But it didn't matter, or she hoped it didn't. Because in the end, she'd made him feel something and that was her heart's greatest wish.

"Well," she said, "you talked yourself into that roll in the hay, smoothie. But then you go get that snake looked at. Deal?"

"You got it, gorgeous."

Now the tech was asking Revv, "Hello? How's that conversation with yourself going?"

"Okay for me. Not so good for the snake."

The tech shook his head. "You're really going to let your pet die?"

"What can I say: I'm coldblooded," Revv said, laughing and howling. "Bowie would have loved that one. He had a superior sense of humor."

But what was this, what kind of stupefying dune of defamation swelled up in him right then? Why was Revv, who had proved immune to guilt and responsibility and liability suddenly feeling like he was doing something wrong? He did tons of things wrong. Hell, he liked doing things wrong, found a contorted pride in flubs and blunders and contusions. Liked to look at the scars on his body and remember all the things he'd done to earn them, fistfights, face plants, mild scrapes with neighborhood kids, etc.

But this... letting Bowie die was something (apparently) that *he* considered wrong. Some secret code of conduct he wasn't aware of, stashed deep in his subconscious, solitary confinement. He thought of a night at Damascus last month: one of the regulars, Karla, sometimes carried a tiny dog in her purse that was no bigger than a burrito. People liked to pet him, feed him peanuts off the bar. He was sort of the joint's unofficial mascot. But on that night, Karla started screaming out of nowhere and people crowded around her and Karla cried and more people crowded and she was yelling and she was holding the tiny dog in her hands, limp and lifeless. It had suffocated in her purse and she hadn't noticed. They all stood gawking at the dead thing. Revv didn't need any help thinking the world was a heartless fiend, so why were all these examples of that clabbered truth circling around him like buzzards?

The detail that bothered him the most was when Karla, still holding the lifeless thing, kept saying, "What am I supposed to do with it? Where does it go? Where does it belong now?"

It was Revv who took it from her. Brought the innocent thing into the office and wrapped it in a bar towel. He asked Karla if she wanted its body, but she said, "Jesus, there's just no way." So he took the wrapped dog out back and put it in the dumpster. Tried to summon some poetic words but could only come up with this brusque eulogy: "I'm sure you didn't deserve to go out like this, pooch. Sorry you got such a poor shake." Then he gave the dog a solemn nod and patted the side of the dumpster.

He'd judged Karla that night, judged her alcoholic tunnel vision, judged her as inept and selfish. He couldn't do something so similar to Bowie. There wouldn't be any honor in this brand of apathy. No, walking away and letting his snake die was the sort of wrongness that didn't jibe with him.

He had to do the right thing.

Begrudgingly, of course.

"Joking, dude," Revv said to the vet tech. "I'm joking. Obviously, I'll shell out the bones to save my Bowie Constrictor. Jeez, give me some credit. I mean, he is my pet after all."

"You sounded pretty serious."

"Just playing."

"Glad to hear it."

"Me, too… I guess," said Revv through gritted teeth.

the dysfunction pub

About an hour after Syl left Revv's, she hooked up with Daph and they were prancing toward Damascus, armed with a greasy bagel—ham, egg, and cheese—to help ease Owen's hangover. Syl was doing her best to recount her night with Revv, the eleven roommates, the impatient sex, the flattened futon, the Jäger machine, the lumpy snake.

"If I may interject," Daph said, "just to clarify, of course. Of the last two gentlemen you've had sexual relations with one called you Harry Potter during coitus and the other is the proud owner of a boa constrictor that ate his boxer shorts?"

As they walked down 24th Street, a man rode a tandem bicycle by himself, sitting on the front seat, ringing a shrill bell on his handlebar and yelling as he passed them, "I'm a good person and a great listener. Would either of you care to join me for a jaunt?"

"No way," they yelled.

That empty backseat was so sad to both women. Syl wondered if this was how he tried to seduce strangers and if it ever succeeded. Unfortunately, she couldn't outright dismiss this as a viable tactic to lure lovers, as she'd once screwed her dental hygienist simply for complimenting her bite. Daph also watched the tandem's bare backseat, except she thought only of Owen: who would ride on the back of his bike besides her, especially if he was dressed like Santa?

The man rang the bell again before pedaling out of earshot, trolling for other women to woo (accost).

The ladies dug back into their conversation. "We didn't know it was boxers at the time," Syl said, "but that's what his text from the vet said."

"Texting, huh? This sounds like more than a one-night stand."

"I'm not wired like you. We're not planning our honeymoon already. He didn't hustle his things into my apartment this morning."

"I can't help that I'm looking for Ms. Right."

"The irony," Syl said, "is that people think I'm the slut. And they're right. But it's okay for you to have ninety-three exes because it's under the guise of looking for true love."

"What a wonderful double-standard!"

"What if I get married before you?"

"Please don't marry Revv," Daph rushed out.

Syl obviously didn't want to marry him, hadn't been specifically talking about Revv, asking the question more in the abstract, but now felt compelled to dig a bit further, seeing as how quickly Daph blurted her answer. "What's wrong with him?"

"Are you joking?

What could she say? She liked 'em rough around the edges. People didn't pick what turned them on. "Revv is better than the guy who said Harry Potter, though, right? It's not his fault the snake was hungry."

"It is if he hadn't fed the poor thing."

"Cut me some slack, please."

"Consider your slack officially cut," Daphne said. "Though I want it put on the record that you're still a bigger slut than I am."

"Maybe."

They were only two blocks from the bar when they bumped into a couple young dykes who had been at the opening of the Olfactory Installation the night before.

"Great work, Syl," one of them said. "That was one of the most meaningful shows I've ever seen."

"It was truly inspired," her friend threw in. "And brave. Aren't you worried about censorship?"

"Why would I be?"

"Animal rights."

Syl hadn't thought much about that, which sounded illogical given the show's extreme premise, but she'd been so immersed in its idea, tunneled way into the core that she hadn't stood back to anticipate public response. Or maybe she had, but only saw rave reviews, pretending the negative prospects were in some kind of blind spot. Maybe that summed up all artists, all people really: she spent her delusions posing in posh, fetishized spotlights, situated far away from any glints of reality that might smirch her fame.

"Embarrassingly," she told them, "that never crossed my mind."

"They say all press is good press," one answered, "so if PETA protests, people will sure know about your show."

"That's true. Thanks for coming out to support us," Syl said.

"We liked your poem," one said to Daph.

"Thanks."

"Keep it up, you two," the women said, staring at Syl, sort of star-struck. Daph felt like an afterthought—an admission of her own—and she probably was. Better to be happy for your friend than to fixate on your brittle ego: nobody seemed to care much for poetry anyway, so she should be happy that the poem even came up. Right? She should be happy with that?

....

A few hours earlier, right after Byron and Sam had left Damascus, Owen peeled himself off of the floor and planted at the bar and drank well whiskey, too cheap to drink the expensive stuff even when he was alone, even given the terrifying circumstances. Sam's warning, the dog tag tattooed on his neck, USMC. Telling Owen he'd be coming back for his eyeball.

Owen's heart had beat more while Sam was in the bar than it had in its entire enterprise. He should have said, "I'll take down the paintings right this second, sir. We can burn them in the street and watch their ashes disappear in the wind. We can give them to charity or pimp them on eBay and you can have all the proceeds. Anything you want, anything at all, just don't hurt me."

This whole thing had started because Owen tried to do the right thing, tried to save Byron from sliding behind the wheel and getting another DUI or killing somebody. Owen tried to help and now he might lose an eye. Yes, he would take the pictures down, he would do what he was told and what he'd promised, but that didn't mean anything, did it? Any man crazy enough to threaten yanking out your eye could renege on a deal in no time. He didn't want to think about it, so he had another pop of well whiskey and wiped his forehead on his Santa suit and took a painting off the wall and set it on the floor.

Don't call the cops.

Don't be a hero.

He took another painting down. He took all twelve down. They were off of the walls and Owen drank well whiskey and eventually he passed out at the bar, in a near narcoleptic episode, no time to toss the sleeping bag onto a pool table and lodge into his gloomy cocoon. Nah, no time for any of that when your forehead crashed down and you were out cold.

Fast forward a few hours and he was still sleeping head down on the bar, and now there was someone knocking on Damascus's door. Poor Owen startled, waking up and his mind going crazy with bashings and frenzies and fluorescent jolts. He'd done what he was supposed to. The paintings were off the walls. Sam could have them. Byron could take an ax to the plywood canvasses. There was no reason to hurt him. I did what you told me to do, Owen would plead. I'm not worth the energy it would take to shatter my bones. I'm not worth cleaning blood from your hands.

Another knock. Knuckles on wood. Heart in your throat. Tears in your eyes.

"Who is it?" Owen yelled.

"We're looking for Santa Claus. We brought him coffee and a bagel for all he does for us kids around the holidays," Daphne said.

"Who's we?"

"Syl's here."

"This is a bad time. Can we talk later?"

"You don't want your coffee?"

"No thanks."

Syl shrugged, then whispered, "Maybe he's got a woman in there," and Daph stuck her tongue out and winced, whispering back, "But you're out here."

"Are you implying I'd screw your uncle?"

"I'm saying you'd screw your uncle."

Owen said, "I'll see you guys later, all right?"

"Okay, weirdo," Daph said, "but I brought you breakfast. At least, let me give it to you."

"Hold on," he said. "Give me a couple of minutes." He rushed over to put the first painting back on the wall, the second, the sixth, the tenth, done. It took about ninety seconds. Some of them were crooked. He wasn't even aware that they'd started to stink, wasn't aware of anything except the looming sense that something terrible was going to happen.

"I'm going to go home," Syl whispered. "This seems like we may be entering the Dysfunction Pub." She hummed the theme song to *The Twilight Zone*.

"I understand," Daphne whispered back, "although I'll judge you harshly and without pity." She made a fist and, like a bully, shook it in front of Syl's face, who pushed it away and walked off, laughing.

The last thing Owen did before opening the front door was

put his Santa beard and hat back on, the latter was a little crusty from being set in a small puddle of white wine before he passed out the night before. He said, "Sorry," and fiddled with the lock and pushed the black door ajar.

He smiled. A façade. He looked like a hostage. Daph had never seen him like this.

"What's wrong with you?" she asked.

Owen adjusted his Santa hat. "I'm fine. Just hungover." He took the bag with the bagel from her. "But I'm in the middle of some things, so can we talk later?"

"What are you in the middle of?"

"It's personal."

"Excuse me?" she said, offended. "It's too personal to tell me?"

"Please."

"We're family."

He shifted the bag to his other hand. "I can't... I don't... please..."

"Can I come in?"

"I don't think that's a good idea."

"Why not?"

He knew that he should refuse, that if she entered Damascus he'd tell her the truth. And Daphne would have an opinion about the matter and she'd share it with him and they'd have to discuss it, and he didn't want to listen because she might think there were options besides simply doing what had been demanded. Daphne was strong and lacked a healthy fear of things that were out of her control.

"You don't want to know," he said.

"Tell me."

He couldn't even do this right, something so simple as shutting a door, locking her out. Was there some prize he'd win if he botched every decision until he was dead?

"Come on in," he said and sighed.

Daph followed him inside.

"Lock the door behind you!" he yelled, startling her.

"Are you in some kind of trouble?"

"If I tell you, promise me you're not going to get involved."

He knew she'd promise. She'd promise and not mean it. He knew he shouldn't tell her, but he was going to do it anyway. Santa was a sucker.

"Uh, okay," she said, "but you're freaking me out a little."

He set the bag on the bar, left the bagel inside of it, poured himself a whiskey.

"Isn't it a little early?" she said.

He shook his head. "Byron was serious."

"About what?"

"He threatened me about Syl's paintings. Told me not to hang them."

"When?"

"Right after he yelled at her yesterday afternoon. He came back last night with a crazy buddy of his. Told me if I didn't take Syl's pictures down before service tonight, he was going to…"—should he mention the eye or stay vague?—"…hurt me."

"Did you call the cops?"

"They specifically told me not to call the cops."

Yes, Byron and Sam had been very clear, but Owen wasn't being so, flailing through his explanation. All his fear and drinking and paranoia were over-spicing the story, overpowering it. He was trying to convince her that there were no options, but all Daphne grasped was how undeniably they needed the help of the police.

This would have been something else that Daph insisted be covered in Owen's admission essay: Owen deserved to be protected, like everybody else. Just because he wasn't always nice to himself didn't mean the rest of the world had the right to gang up on him.

"We have to call the cops," she said. "This is what they do."

"And if they scare them away tonight, so what? There's next Wednesday, a week from Friday—who's going to save me when he pulls out my eye?"

"Your eye?"

"It's a figure of speech."

"I know you want to listen to what they said, but you deserve the cops' protection."

Don't give in, Owen begged himself. Don't cave. Don't let her intellectualize this. She wasn't there. She didn't see Sam.

"What if they don't keep me safe?"

"I'm sure the cops deal with situations like this all the time."

"You're sure?"

"I'm reasonably sure."

"Oh, Jesus, *reasonably* sure," Owen said. "This is getting better by the second."

As though there was any doubt, Daphne won the "argument," promising that the police would keep Owen safe, that she understood his fear of short-term versus long-term consequences, the phobia that the fracas would kick down his front door and demand retribution after the cops had again left Damascus; but, as she explained it to him, they didn't have a choice: Byron and his friend would probably come back whether the paintings were removed or not. They were acting like crazy people and needed to be treated as though they were capable of anything. Owen and Daph weren't prepared to handle that sort of thing. It was better to alert those paid to protect us, trained in such matters.

"You," Daph said to him, "are too important to take chances with."

He sighed.

"Can I call them now?" she said.

"You didn't see how scary they were."

"We can't deal with this on our own."

"I thought Byron was my friend."

"Sounds like he needs some help."

"I bought him fig bars."

"Can I call the cops?"

He sighed again, nodded, duped by his niece, strength lopped off by his love for her. According to Byron, all Santa had to do was listen, which seemed like a simple instruction, but these elusive senses of his had been forfeit, obscured for so long that he didn't know where to search. He slugged another cheap whiskey while she dialed the police.

"I want to be buried in my Santa suit," he said.

even the high road bottoms out

No Eyebrows sipped schnapps at a bar six blocks from Damascus the day after the art show. It was early afternoon, and aside from him, the joint was empty. That was until the door opened, and a guy walked in and sat down on the barstool right next to No Eyebrows. Uncouth protocol. Barstools were like urinals: you never sidled right up next to someone unless there were no other slots available.

After about thirty seconds the newcomer said, "I know why the whales keep beaching themselves." He scratched at a vicious case of eczema on his forearms and with each raking of his nails, dead skin snowed like someone was wildly grating parmesan cheese. "Evolution, man. They want to walk, breathe, buy stocks. They want to be the next dominant land species. Soon we'll all kneel at the feet of the whales."

Currently, No Eyebrows waited for Shambles to arrive for their "deeper deliberation" (her words, whatever the hell they meant). She'd said to him after Syl's Olfactory Installation, "I need... we need a deeper deliberation of what we're doing here."

He tried to lighten things up: "Are you sure you want to deliberate with me? I'm a lawyer."

"I need to hear more about you," she said, and he agreed, and now here he was, listening to a rabidly scratching man talk about the ever-evolving motives of whales.

In a weird way No Eyebrows was happy to placate the guy, indulge in distracting dialogue, a bastion from Shambles, his dividing cells, and abandoned family. "Wait, whales have feet?" he asked the itchy scientist.

"Feet will be a crucial part of their evolution, yes." In addition to his violent scratching attacks, he wore yellow-tinted glasses and had a habit of looking at whomever he spoke to over the tops of the rims, leaning his chin down, like a haughty professor. He had on a dirty V-neck sweater, sleeves rolled up to his elbows, and he wore his receding blond hair slicked straight back. Three or four days of stubble on his face, mostly gray. He smelled like sweat and butterscotch.

"Interesting theory," No Eyebrows said.

"Hey, don't forget we crawled out of the ocean, too. Humankind, Cro-Magnon, Homo erectus, monkey... we used to be frogs, man. Before that we swam around, gilled and armless and stupid."

"They better hurry up and sprout legs, or it all might end before their grand entrance."

"They're trying to accelerate evolution. Some have to die for the greater good." He coughed, scratched again, more dead skin skydiving to the bar, some catching a bit of wind and snaking in No Eyebrows' ear.

"Will you buy me a beer?" the itchy scientist said.

No Eyebrows flagged down the bartender, ordered the man a Pabst Blue Ribbon because it was the cheapest, and paid.

"Thanks," the man said, sipping. "Once the whales are here, things will be different. No more of this sad carnival."

"What makes you such an expert?"

"Research. I've hitchhiked all up and down the West Coast. I try and make it to every single site where a beaching has occurred. I look for clues, answers. Remember, it wasn't that long ago that everyone thought the earth was flat."

"It was pretty long ago."

"Not in the true scheme, it wasn't."

"I guess," No Eyebrows said. "Isn't it scary hitchhiking?"

"Not for me. I was an army ranger. Still am, really. Once they program you, it's in your hard drive for good. I can kill a man with his own eyelashes."

"If you can do that, I'm glad all my hair fell out."

"You have cancer?"

"Most people don't ask me that directly."

"How do they ask?"

"They just stare."

"Thanks for the Pabst," the itchy scientist said. "I like Heineken. They make a better beer over in Europe. Something to do with their water supply and stellar bottling tactics. I don't know. Pabst tastes like they got the water from Lake Michigan. I always check the bottom of the bottle to make sure there are no used condoms floating in there."

"You're welcome."

"I understand your skepticism about the whales. I used to lack faith, too."

"God led you to the whales?"

"No, I think the whales led me to god, but who really knows what guides any of us anywhere, right?"

No Eyebrows hadn't been the first to throw in the towel on his existence. His oncologist, after the last PET and CAT scans showed the new tumors on his spine, said, "I don't think your body can handle any more chemo."

"So what do we do?"

But the doctor just shook his head.

"That's it?" No Eyebrows asked.

"Enjoy the time you have left. Be with your family."

He made it sound so easy...

Back in the bar, No Eyebrows said to his new friend, "So what clues have you found at the beachings?"

His excitement made him scratch his forearms harder, a blizzard now: "These whales aren't trying to get back to the water. They're trying to get farther up the beach."

"Sure that's not due to the tide?"

"Tide? What do you take me for? Tide? I'm a student of the ocean, for god's sake."

"My apologies," No Eyebrows said. "I shouldn't have questioned your methodology."

"When the whales run the world, there won't be any more cynicism. Won't even be citizenship to countries. We'll be one people and won't squabble over crumbs like famished vultures. We'll have important reasons to live and when was the last time any of us felt like that?"

No Eyebrows remembered the first afternoon he found out about the cancer. The dramatic speech he gave his wife about *beating this damn thing*. Remembered that he'd even said things as arrogant as he wouldn't allow himself to die, not yet, he loved his family too much and there was no way he'd let some disease take all this happiness away.

"I have reasons to live," No Eyebrows said to the scientist, "but the world doesn't seem to care."

"That's bringing the hammer down on the nail. We're as hollow as bamboo."

"Are you ready for that Heineken?"

"Is a whale ready to evolve?"

•••••••

Twenty minutes later, the wayward, itchy scientist was telling No Eyebrows a dirty joke—one about the difference between a midget and a mud puddle—but he hushed before the punch line, as Shambles walked in. She gave the place the once-over. A bunch of people had arrived since No Eyebrows first entered. Shambles never trusted this place, Drunk Again, with all its manic outcasts: addicts recently escaped from their last attempts at sobriety (the bathroom always had the burned tinfoil reek from tar heroin); people drinking with hospital bracelets on, sometimes still wearing the garb issued to them from SF General, bandages covering their wounds from fights, falling, self-mutilation, gangrenous tears from needles; those in the midst of benders, liquor muting the volume of stale woes, a reality void of afflictions: *what you can't remember, can't hurt you...*; the homeless drank at this dump, too, fifty cent pints of PBR served until five p.m. bought with the money they'd received from recycling bottles and cans or panhandling, their empty shopping carts parked out front of the bar, like horses in the old west.

And, of course, the next generation of alcoholics, the reinforcements, twenty-two, twenty-six, thirty-four years old, who came of age admiring Kerouac, Bukowski, Burroughs, early Tom Waits. Turned on by their seductive tales of debauchery. They didn't fathom that the movie *Barfly* wasn't real, didn't understand that they'd never meet Faye Dunaway while drinking bourbon in the afternoon. They didn't know about years of diarrhea, of ulcers, anal fissures and hemorrhoids and shaking hands and dementia and memory uncoiling and nightmares and night-sweats and hangovers so brutally majestic you kneeled before them and wept.

"It was nice chatting with you," No Eyebrows said to the whale-lover and scooted down the bar, onto a new stool next to Shambles, saying to her, "Don't ask."

"I wasn't going to."

"Don't you wanna hear the rest of the joke?" the itchy scientist called down, still grating his forearm-cheese with every rake of fingernail.

"No, thanks."

"Let me know if you change your mind."

"Shall do."

The bartender asked Shambles what was her poison, and she answered, "I'll take a rusty nail, please." He sighed and rolled his eyes, seeming really put out by this request.

"Is that a problem?" she asked.

"Lady, the guy who taught me to tend bar had a saying: a good drink has two ingredients, and one of them is ice."

"I'll still take a rusty nail, though I do apologize for making you do your job," she said.

The bartender muttered and slunk away. He saw drunkards as nothing more than cheap beef. You hear about this phenomenon with surgeons or EMTs or cops, people who see too much damage, too many pulpy human disgraces. It happened in the bar business, too. You couldn't care about the customers while witnessing such opulent self-destruction.

"How are you doing?" she said to No Eyebrows.

He tried to smile. "I'm not dead yet."

"Does that answer my question?"

"Sort of."

The bartender sloshed her rusty nail on the bar. The itchy scientist played a couple songs on the jukebox and danced alone in slow circles, scratching his sloughing arms, mouthing the words to an old David Bowie song.

"I'm sorry I couldn't talk at Damascus last night," she said. "I didn't know what to say."

"About what?"

"Our cab ride."

"Ah, right."

"You scared me."

"I shouldn't have invited you back to my room," he said, though he knew what he wanted, why he'd asked: his wife used to spoon him in bed, wrapped herself around him, his skinny butt like a hot water bottle pressed against her stomach. He used to get so overheated and annoyed trying to sleep like that, their sweaty bodies mashed together, yet he craved to be held like that now. What a luxury, those sorts of domestic aggravations...

"You don't need to apologize," Shambles said, brushing her spangled bangs to the side. "I didn't know what to do with all of it."

"All what?"

"Those things you said. Dying babies in German orphanages

and that you left your family. How you needed someone to touch you."

"Someone did touch me."

She sipped her rusty nail. "Were you already married when you got sick?"

"Yes."

"And you have a daughter."

"I can't talk about this."

"Well, I can't be here with you unless we talk about you leaving them."

No Eyebrows stopped, didn't let himself say anything because his instinct was to leave. To get as far away from this conversation as possible. If any woman deserved an explanation, her name was Sally and she was over the Golden Gate Bridge in Mill Valley. She was the mother of his only child. She was his best friend. She was his love. She was perfect. And he left her anyway, didn't see an alternative. Things were already getting so bad in his body and they would only get worse. "I didn't want her to know any of the specifics," he said to Shambles. "She can know it in the abstract, but I won't allow her to have these memories."

"Is that entirely your decision to make?"

"They're entirely my tumors."

"She must be devastated," Shambles said and sipped her rusty nail.

"Thanks for pointing that out."

"I'm just saying she must really be worried."

"I know this makes me a bad person. But staying there… staying with them hurt too much."

Shambles was shocked. "Do you want to keel over dead in Damascus, a bunch of strangers stepping over you to get some free peanuts off the bar?"

"I'd prefer that, yeah."

"You're an idiot."

"Is this why you wanted to meet me today?" He was ready to get up and leave and never see her again. They were his tumors, damnit, and it was his decision and who the hell did this woman think she was? Did she think it was easy for him to leave? Was she really that dense? He could have stayed and it might have been even worse than he'd imagined: month after month after month of incrementally disappearing, one dividing cell at a time.

"I'm sorry," Shambles said, recognizing she might have gone a step too far, but she wanted to understand his decision, its logic. She couldn't save him, but maybe she could pick up the screaming baby and whisper that everything was going to be okay, even if that was a skyscraping lie. "I'm always thinking about you. As I'm going to sleep, I can hear everything you said that night in the cab, echoing around my apartment. A couple times I even got up and looked around to see if you were there. It's silly, I know. I have no idea what I'm doing here. I'm sorry I couldn't answer anything you said in the taxi. Sorry I couldn't sleep in your bed."

"You don't need to apologize."

"I'm not judging you, just trying to understand," she said and finished her rusty nail.

He touched her hand. "I judge me enough for the both of us."

"Have you been thinking about me?"

"I'm the one who keeps coming to see you, remember?"

She hadn't remembered. Or she only remembered things that verified her fear that she wanted to be with him more than he wanted to be with her. She wasn't worried about anything rational; she worried about this bemusing compulsion to soak up every second she could with him, her cancer patient. If he was dying soon, she wanted to witness the rest of his days. If he'd allow a final visitor. If a man condemned to death didn't want his family to observe his execution, she wanted to be his surrogate.

But it wasn't that simple, either. He was making the wrong

choice. He was doing something selfish and terrible, and it didn't seem like he was going to recognize that on his own.

Shambles looked up at the ceiling. All of the building's support beams were exposed, painted white, aligned in straight rows. Looked like a giant ribcage, like they were inside someone.

They finished their drinks; he ordered another round. Another Bowie song came on. A slower one. "Will you dance with me?" Shambles said.

"I can't dance."

"So what? Do you think these deadbeats even know what day it is?"

He hesitated, hoping he didn't fall down in the middle of the song. Pretty woozy. His oncologist had told him that ultimately he'd need to wear an eye-patch to steady his equilibrium, as the tumor continued to manhandle his cerebellum. He closed one eye. It sturdied him some. He'd have to keep it cinched the whole time they danced.

"Let's cut the rug," he said.

"What rug? This is concrete."

No Eyebrows stood up, extended his hand to her, and she took it. Hers much warmer. They walked into the middle of the room, the middle of the ribcage, and danced, two people dancing. They didn't talk to each other while they moved. Neither wanted to. They were in each other's arms and that was enough. It was everything. He hadn't lied about being an awful dancer, but she didn't care.

She rested her head on his shoulder and felt the portacath jetting from his skin. She apologized for bumping it, and he said it was fine, didn't hurt, don't worry, please keep your head there. She did. And her mind zoomed to another cancer patient, this one a cancer survivor: Shambles had met her at Burning Man last year, the first morning on the Playa. The woman was easily over 300 pounds, completely nude and sitting cross-legged, like a Buddha. She had endured a double-mastectomy, scars stretching over her missing breasts. She sat there, eyes closed, for everyone to examine. People surrounded her; people celebrated her; people surrendered to her like she was a work of art. And she was.

Shambles had asked the woman's permission to snap some photos of her, and she agreed. After Burning Man, Shambles printed hard copies and mounted them into an album. She viewed them weekly, often daily; they became a kind of worship.

This memory made Shambles' mind connect dots in a weird way. Grasping at straws, maybe. Sure, she couldn't literally save No Eyebrows. His cells would not be salvaged. But maybe she could save him from something else: the mistake he was making with his family. She could imagine his wife, broken down, no other way to cope with your lover's disappearance but to fold into yourself and sob until there wasn't a drop of water left in your body, leaving you ravaged, dehydrated, skin and bones, just like him.

He needed to see the photographs, the woman's ornate scars.

The first person to speak was the itchy scientist, shimmying next to them in his incarcerating circles; his spinning motions and his forearm scratches made his dead skin whirl around him like a harmless tornado. "Can you feel it?" he said.

No Eyebrows didn't say anything. His eye still shut. This felt better than any other time they'd touched.

"Feel what?" Shambles felt obligated to ask.

"We're in the belly of the whale, man. We've been swallowed whole."

Maybe she had been swallowed whole, but it had nothing to do with any whale. Her head still rested against No Eyebrows' portacath. Shambles tilted to look up at the ceiling again, the white beams like ribs stretching across the entire room, further even, across their whole lives. She knew what she had to do.

the occupation (erotic sedition)

The Right Hand of the law was right here. The Right Hand was in Damascus, as the bar opened for business that evening. Two undercovers bellied up. After consulting with the police, this was what they recommended: an unstated presence to be kept on the premises for a few days to suss things out and evaluate the threat.

Theoretically, this should have assuaged Owen's fear of impending retaliation. It did not. They did not. This particular Right Hand of the law wasn't instilling much confidence in the skeptical barkeep, though they spoke with pomp and dazzle: "No shit's going down on our watch; we're a couple mean motherfuckers," one of them had said as he plopped onto a barstool and ordered a soda pop with a maraschino cherry.

Daphne had nailed a black basket to Damascus's front door and filled it with surgical masks. A sign above it said: *Come smell our art show. Masks are optional, but recommended.* This was another point the police had made: let the perpetrators perceive that business was continuing on as though there had been no ripple made. The illusion of the status quo. The bait of having not taken the bait.

The Right Hand themselves had refused surgical masks upon entering Owen's domain on the grounds that one of them had a better way of blocking the bar's fertile death-stench. "This is how we did it in 'Nam," he said, breaking an unfiltered cigarette in half and shoving a slim stalk up each of his nostrils. "It'll stop any smell, no matter how foul."

"No shit?"

"For real."

"You shittin' me?" his partner said, stunned, a wondrous look on his face.

"Nope."

The enamored partner asked him for an unfiltered smoke, snapped it in two, shoved the halves up his nose as well. He sniffed deeply, then smiled: "Everything smells like cigarettes. I should've done this yeeeeaaaarrrrs ago."

The bar's god-awful pungency had given Owen a respite from the rumbling in his head since calling the cops. He could still feel the sear of Byron's betrayal and see Sam's USMC carved in his neck.

Soon a sad chap stumbled into the bar, holding his surgical mask, his face wincing as he registered the rotting smell, holding his nose with his free hand. "How the hell am I supposed to drink while wearing this mask?"

"Don't you ever watch TV?" one of the cops said, cigarette wedges still fitted in his nostrils. "Dramas based in the chaotic environment of emergency rooms? You only tie the top strings. Let the lower ones dangle free, like overcooked French fries. That way you can slip your drink under it."

"A-ha," the sad chap said, relieved, pulling his arms behind his head and blindly tying the bow and falling onto a barstool like a jetlagged passenger might crash-land on a mattress, tired and relieved and exactly where he wanted to be.

The cops shook their heads and requested refills of their sodas.

"Do I watch doctor-dramas?" the sad chap said. "If that's what you're asking me, I can guarantee you that the answer is hell no. I've got better things to do with my time besides watching handsome, muscle-bound doctors seduce doe-eyed nurses in the operating room."

"They're not all that predictable," the cop said.

"Who said anything about predictable? It just so happens that my ex-wife was one of those doe-eyed nurses, and I don't need to waste any more of my time, thank you very much, remembering that handsome, muscle-bound doctors steal people's doe-eyed wives while they're driving a truck from San Diego to Tacoma."

Owen, like any veteran bartender, knew the best way to handle the sad chap was to ask him what he'd like to drink, first one's on the house, friend, no need to worry, we understand your plight.

To which the wounded newcomer could only say, "I mean, a spinal surgeon. How'm I supposed to compete with a spinal surgeon?"

Quiet from the sad chap for a few minutes, muttering only to his drink and then this narcotic non sequitur: "Hey, anybody wanna do some blow?"

He pulled a little plastic baggie from his pocket, dabbing at its outside with a paper napkin. "I got it kinda sticky, but I'm nipping that issue in the bud. If only Janice could see me now, taking the bull by the horns, cleaning this thing off all by myself." He carefully wiped the baggie like it was a baby bird smeared in oil after a tanker spill.

"Listen, those guys are cops," Owen said to him.

"The ones with smokes up their noses?"

"Yeah."

"On or off duty?" he asked the cops.

"On," they grumbled. "Put that shit away."

"You know what? I suddenly realize that I need to relieve myself and think I'll hit the head in order to do so. How's that sound, gentlemen? Everyone on board with that decision? I'll be making my way to the restroom now and minding my own business from here on out. Thanks very much for your time, gentlemen," the sad chap said and retired to the restroom.

At exactly 5:19 p.m.—while he was doing a bump of coke

off his apartment key—Damascus's front door opened and an army of people marched in, manning their surgical masks. Ten, thirty, fifty. Weird thing was, not one person approached the bar, instead walking from portrait to portrait, admiring Syl's work.

"No one ordered a drink," Owen said to Daphne.

"They will. Let them soak up Syl's paintings first."

A loud voice boomed from outside. No one in Damascus knew it was a megaphone yet. At first, everyone looked around and squinted their confused faces. But the voice, a female's, shouted from out front, "1-2-3-4, we don't want your racist war! 5-6-7-8, the US is a terror-state!"

Owen was the first to investigate, storming outside, not worried about Byron or Sam because the voice's message didn't sound like anything they'd ever support. It in fact sounded like the sort of heresy they seemed charged to seek out and stomp. Owen was used to chasing clogged idiots away from the front of his bar as they were in the midst of making scenes—mawkish couples screaming at each other, alpha man-boys standing around and grab-assing, clusters of kids huddled and puffing joints—but as he swung open the door... there were a hundred people standing on the sidewalk, some hoisting signs, others yelling in pure call and response back at their inspired instigator: "...5-6-7-8, the US is a terror-state!"

"What do we want?" she said.

"Justice!" they screamed.

"When do we want it?"

"Now!"

Owen, dumbfounded, turned around and bolted back into his man-made universe. The first protester to enter Damascus was a young man carrying a sign that said, *No casualties for oil* followed by the more laconic *Fascist America* followed by a girl toting *George W. Bush is guilty of war crimes.*

Owen was once again behind the bar. People poured in the front door, packing the place, all wearing the surgical masks.

More people than had ever been in the bar. Way beyond maximum capacity. He hoped the fire marshal was out of town.

The Inspired Instigator finally came in and said into her megaphone, "I don't know if there are any Republicans in the bar, but if so, you're complicit in every murder done on your behalf. Your vote means you pull the trigger, drop the bomb. Your vote for George W. Bush makes you a monster, too."

Owen leaned over to Daphne and asked, "Should I be concerned?"

All she did was smile at him and say, "You should be proud."

....

Syl and Revv took a taxi to Damascus, right after Daph had called and told them about the protest. They walked in as the Inspired Instigator asked everyone, "What's the difference between *preemptive* and *unprovoked*?"

"Spelling!" they all shouted.

"What's the difference?"

"Spelling!"

Syl's smile grew as all these people yelled their unified protests. Her artwork had been its own megaphone: the years of tormenting anonymity had been worth it; her twenties were worth it; every time she spoke to her parents and they asked how "her little art hobby" was going; every time she spoke with her older brother, who somehow always reminded her of his MBA, his mortgage, his fiscal success, by simply inquiring if it was time to "get a job and mitigate her struggles." (Family members always knew the routes to our most delicate wounds.) None of that mattered anymore. Each anonymous day that had preceded yesterday, her Olfactory Installation, had simply been practice, honing her skills, and now she was out on her high wire, making her way between the Towers, veering into artistic heights she'd never thought real, a vantage point so encompassing that she was able to slander our crumbling empire. Smell our war, she reminded everyone. Smell our dissipating future. Smell

America's international reputation. Smell the smeared blood on George W. Bush's hands. Smell the shit on Dick Cheney and Donald Rumsfeld and Condoleezza Rice. Smell the shit in Iraq, in Afghanistan. Smell our shitty arrogance. Smell every shitty citizen. Smell us.

And hopefully her show was about more than Iraq: hopefully, Syl's show talked about Vietnam and the World Wars and Korea and the Cold War and all the skirmishes that got buried in history's footnotes (will Iraq be one of those casualties?), like Panama and Grenada and Beirut and El Salvador and Libya and Haiti and the Philippines and Mexico and the next dozen brawls. The average American citizen followed what happened in the Middle East and Afghanistan with a vague, annoyed interest. This was her kill-shot: all the privileged ennui. All of *your* privileged ennui.

Daphne came up to Syl and said, "You, Ms. Sylvia Suture, have arrived." Then Daph shoved back through the crowd and jumped up onto the bar, much to Owen's Santa-bearded dismay. "May I have your attention, please?" she asked Damascus. "Hey. Shut up! I'd like to introduce you all to Sylvia Suture, the mastermind and featured artist. Get up here, girl."

Syl climbed onto the bar as Daphne got down. Applause, deafening and long lasting, followed by absolute silence as they waited for her to say something. "Those of you who are wearing surgical masks, take them off. Let's all have a whiff through our noses. The deepest breath your lungs can handle. Let's smell the death and think about every unnecessary casualty."

Unmasked, everybody breathed deeply.

Like a group of high school seniors completing graduation and tossing their caps in the air, everyone in Damascus threw their surgical masks skyward, an unpolluted denunciation. The masks sashayed to the ground slowly, tiny parachutes.

Syl hopped off of the bar and hugged Daphne, kissed Revv. For him, this was erotic sedition. She might as well have been naked and burning the American flag. It made him wonder whether he could have that kind of commitment to his music. So far, he'd gummed things up as much as the other guys in his half-assed bands. He'd start another one ASAP and write songs to smash the kneecaps of the oppressors. A life without art was like skin without tattoos, boring and empty and pale.

Then Owen said to all, "This round of drinks is on the house," which he had never done before, buying a cocktail for the whole lot. Forget appearances: he was acting like Santa Claus, too.

••••••••

At a certain point in the evening, each guest eloquently drenching their psyches in their favorite spirits, NASCAR races running fast laps inside their skulls, everything went back to normal.

A man pushed his way to the bar, toward Owen, and said, "Do you know your way around this neighborhood pretty well?"

"Absolutely," Owen said. "What are you looking for?"

"A place called Smart Fuckers. You ever heard of it?" He wore a black collared shirt with embroidered roses all over it. Black hair pasted back. A shaggy flavor-savor beneath his bottom lip, kinked hairs sticking out from it every which way like an anemone's tentacles.

"Excuse me?"

"Smart Fuckers. You know anything about it?"

Reflexively, Owen looked over at the cops, but they weren't watching him; the bar's capacity and incessant commotion had sort of worn down the Right Hand's perceptions, both washed out and overtired, things seeming normal enough for them to talk between themselves, smokes still up their noses. Owen would have to yell to get their attention. So shouldn't he be yelling? Jesus, it felt impossible to make noise.

"I don't want any trouble," Owen said to the man.

"You must want trouble," he said, "because you didn't listen to what he told you. Why didn't you follow his instructions?"

"The police are here."

"We know that." Then he screamed at the top of his lungs, "Infestation!"

Fifteen men, all distributed throughout the crowd, not identifiable by any uniformity in their clothing or ethnicity or mood, now poised themselves to strike. Fifteen consciences ranging from troubled to resigned to comatose. A motley stash of renegades without much continuity amongst their motives—certainly some were there because of the egregious act of the artist's portraits and Owen's unwillingness to follow Sam's instructions. They represented the core, the top tier, zealots, those touched as intimately as Byron—*it could be me, man. I could be hanging on your wall!* These fundamentalists were repulsed and ready for revenge.

Some henchmen comprised the second tier and were drinking buddies with Sam, who had a kind of brutal charisma, convincing and roping acquaintances into petty crimes (larceny, assault, slinging drugs) even back before his time in the service. These were "half-believers," here as mercenaries to muscle up and deal with crowd control.

The last subdivision, the third tier, were those orbiting around *the reason!* from the greatest distance, like the last couple planets, Uranus and Neptune, way out yonder from the sun yet still ruled by its gravitational pull. Simply here for hire, they were contracted to intimidate by proxy, standing around and growling to deter any bravery from wandering onto the stage.

Once the man yelled, "Infestation!" the occupation began in earnest. Two henchmen who had been stationed directly behind the Right Hand struck first, pulling out canisters of pepper spray and leaning around and getting each of the cops dead in the eyes, then shoving them onto the floor and kicking them, handcuffing them, covering their mouths in duct tape (three of the four cigarette wedges fell from their nostrils, only one remained snug). The rest of the cronies pulled goggles from their pockets, put them on, and yanked out their own canisters of pepper spray, misting the toxic aerosol into the air.

Chaos!

Anarchy!

People screaming, tearing, blinded, stumbling. People in every corner of Damascus panicking and whimpering.

The henchmen rustled and ushered all of the bar's customers into one half of Damascus, situated over by the pool tables. They confiscated purses and bags and cell phones and wallets and jackets and the megaphone. They demanded everyone get down on the floor, sit Indian-style, hold their arms up in the air. Shut up and no one's gonna get hurt, okay?

Some of the henchmen penned the hostages off by forming a human fence, standing armed with pepper spray, some wielding telescoping billy clubs that had been fastened to their thighs. They were the only division between the hostages and what was about to happen. Their omnipotence dared any of the blinded prisoners to do anything extraordinary, ordinary, desperate. Dared them to do anything except sit there with burning eyes.

The guy who had been talking to Owen pulled out a cell phone and after a few seconds said into it, "Time to pay the piper," and a minute later, the front door opened, Sam and Byron wearing goggles of their own, invading Damascus and standing in the middle of the room, under the man-made stars and clouds.

A sign that said *Private Party* was tacked to the bar's front door. The remaining surgical masks and the corresponding invitation to employ one were removed. The door was locked.

Sam stormed over to the prisoners and found Owen, said, "Hey, Santa, you don't have to sit with the peasants. You're the king. Get over here." He stroked his long goatee, scratched his dog tag tattoo. He'd escaped the Sane Asylum, free from the rules and truces and passivity.

One of the third-tier mercenaries, living way on the outskirts from *the reason!* and doing this for 200 measly dollars and regretting this decision more with every second, retrieved a still-blinded Owen from the pen and guided him to the bar, helped him plunk onto a stool.

"What do you want?" Owen said to Sam.

But Byron came over close to Owen and answered, "Why can't you just listen to what I told you?"

"Please don't do this."

"Pardon my colleague," Sam said to Owen, marching over. "I'm afraid Byron's a bit partial to you, which as you can imagine makes him conflicted about our current brouhaha."

"You made me do this," Byron said and looked at Owen, who only nodded in agreement—he couldn't argue: they said don't rile the troops, and that was what Owen had done. He felt dumber than ever and that was saying something.

Sam glared through his goggles at Byron, then addressed Owen, "Now, you asked what I want... well, I want what we agreed upon last night. I'm here to collect what's mine."

"Please," said Owen. "Don't do this."

"I've got a new plan. You're going to love this." Then Sam spoke to everybody in the bar, "Listen, we are not here to hurt you or rob you. We will not take anyone's money. Your valuables will be returned to you in full; you have my word on that. We are here because your humble Santa Claus didn't want to follow some very simple instructions." Sam retrieved the woman's megaphone from the pile of confiscated merchandise and spoke into it: "Until we leave, your First Amendment rights have been temporarily cancelled. From here on out, you have only one right: the right to remain silent, and if you choose to breach it, I'll break your fucking jaw myself."

No one said anything, just muffled prayers, tears.

"Good," Sam said. "Now, I know the artist is present. Where is she? Where is this politico?"

Syl stiffened; Daphne stiffened; Owen stiffened; Revv stiffened.

"I'm going to need her help with what comes next," Sam was saying. "Help her, boys. Help her up here so we can kick off the real beginning of the show."

A mid-tier mercenary pulled Syl to the middle of Damascus, left her standing with Sam and Byron, Owen only a few feet away sitting at the bar, everybody else trapped in the makeshift prison.

"Nice to meet you," Sam said to Syl.

She didn't answer.

"Cat got your tongue?"

Nothing.

"Maybe you can paint that next," he said. "A woman with a cat in her mouth."

Still nothing.

"We're about to see how smart this fucker really is," Sam said to his caged audience.

the hazy illusion of healing

Where are we going?" No Eyebrows asked Shambles, after they'd finished dancing in the dive bar.

"My apartment."

"Why?"

"I want to show you something." Shambles said her place wasn't far and that they could take a cab if walking a few blocks was too daunting for him, which made him feel feeble and useless, which made him remember that he was indeed feeble and useless, and now he wanted to sulk in a corner of this rank joint and drink a bottle of schnapps.

"I hate this," he said.

"What?"

"That walking a few blocks is a challenge."

"You don't need to be embarrassed when I'm around."

"I'm not. I'm embarrassed when I'm around," he said.

They made their way outside. A sort of sidewalk food co-op had sprouted since they'd been in the bar. One woman sold homemade tamales and empanadas from a small cart. Another offered plates of *dulce de leche* from a card table. A man flung hotdogs wrapped in bacon from a sizzling pan.

It was windy. In his younger days No Eyebrows disliked—really despised—the wind because it messed up his hair. He was one of those men who'd kept a full head of it into his late forties and was damn proud, found an immense pleasure in combing its black and gray swirl, styling it with product.

When the oncologist had told him that all his body hair would fall out during chemo, No Eyebrows decided to have a barber preemptively shave his head bald, rather than endure watching clumps of it fall from his scalp and scatter around the house. He couldn't bring himself to go to his usual stylist, so he found some crappy barber that only charged $8 and didn't offer any of the bourgeois pampering that he'd grown accustomed to: no glass of champagne or scalp massage or shampoo and conditioning, etc. No, this was just a wrinkled man lucky to live into his sixties apathetically chopping every follicle from No Eyebrows' head. It was a gruff, sad transaction: *I take your full head of hair; you give me a meager $8 and don't tip; we never see each other again.*

And now he almost appreciated the wind since it couldn't tousle his vanity. It was yet another thing he'd only experience for a little while longer, and in that sense, it was something else to miss.

"You're quite a dancer," he said to her.

"You're quite a charmer. Am I walking too fast?"

"This is fine." The wind blew her hair and he watched her hair blow and he thought of his bald head. "I used to have quite a mane."

"Did you?"

"Handsome," he said. "Dare I say that I was handsome?"

....

"It's official," Shambles' husband said, her ex-husband. This was over the phone, of course. Of course, they were talking over the phone because seeing each other in person would be too personal, and personally she didn't want that. "We're divorced," he said, feigning exhilaration. "I got the final papers in the mail. Isn't this exciting?"

"Another joke. Now that we're divorced, I almost find you funny again."

"I'll never understand..."

"Understand what?"

"What was wrong with our marriage? We knew each other well. We were nice; we were respectful. Our apartment was great. It was a solid arrangement."

"Too routine."

"You use the word 'routine' like it's a disease," he said.

"To me, it is."

"You're always so dramatic. So now what: how are you going to live now? What will be your first adventure so you never have to endure another routine?"

"More jokes," she said. "A perfect way to end things. I don't want every day to be the same as the one before it. I'm not asking for *extra*ordinary, just not the same ordinary day after day."

"Let me get this straight: you're looking for a variety of ordinariness?"

"You can have your jokes, and I can have my delusions," she said to him. "How does that sound?"

"Fine, I guess. But they're both jokes. Right now you're telling a better joke than I ever did: different kinds of ordinary: that doesn't exist."

"It does so."

"It doesn't."

"It does."

"No," he said, "it doesn't."

"We'll see," she said.

And she did see, though she never called to tell him he was right.

•••••••

"I want to show you some photographs," Shambles said to No Eyebrows as they sat in her living room.

"Of what?"

"A woman."

"Is she naked?" he joked.

"She is." Shambles retrieved the photo album from the other

room and returned clutching it to her chest. "I don't have any schnapps but would you like a whiskey?"

"Please."

Still clutching the album, she walked into the kitchen. Shambles set it down, made them drinks, tucked the album under her arm and returned carrying everything. Then she handed him one of the whiskies.

"To us," she said sadly, forgetting her liver and shin splints.

"To us."

They drank, set their glasses down.

"Here," she said and gave him the album, "but don't open it yet."

"Okay."

"I want to explain this." If only she knew this woman from Burning Man, could introduce the two of them. If only there could be a meeting, if only the woman could clutch him, hold him right up to her scars and they could tell him a thousand secrets that would ease his burden, that flamboyant anger that slopped through him. "This woman is sick, too," she said, "and I want you to see her body."

"Why?"

"Because she's beautiful. And you're beautiful."

He stood up. "I have to go."

"Don't."

"Why do you care?"

"She's still alive," Shambles said.

"Pass on my congratulations." Same old shit as when they'd been in the bar, same old badgering scheme. Shambles' heart, he supposed, was in the right place. He didn't think there was malice here, but misguided "help" could be malicious—it could accost you.

"You say you left because you didn't want them to watch," Shambles said, "but you don't even know when you're going to die."

"I won't make it."

"What if it's months from now?"

"So what?"

"That's a long time. Why not be with them?" she asked, her own marriage maneuvering to the forefront of her mind. She'd grown tired of being soldered into a blasé routine. Fastened so that each day was the same day as the last. But was there anything really wrong with that? They had the one thing No Eyebrows didn't have—time to fix it. And if she was bored with her ex, yet he was happy bobbing in stagnant water, couldn't they adapt? If there was a lesson to learn from that day at Jenner, at the beach, their sandy foundation giving way underneath them, maybe it was that you had to keep your feet moving.

No Eyebrows was on the verge of tears. "It isn't a long time. It's nothing."

She walked to him, hugged him, kissed him; he did not want her this close, not right then. "Please sit with me," Shambles said.

"What's the point?"

"She's still alive, and so are you."

He'd skim, he decided, glance at a couple photos, and shut the album. He'd give her that much because he knew her intentions were good, but she had no god damn idea what she was talking about, months were nothing, weeks were nothing.

They planted on the couch together. He picked up the album, opened it, glanced at the first photo. Then really looked at it. There the large woman was, nude and sweaty. Huge scars where her breasts had been. And the most unbelievable detail: she was smiling.

On her face. A smile.

Mesmerized.

Transported…

And do you know what he thought of? Costco. That last trip. When he had to sit down on the concrete and had to be wheeled over near the exit by the employee. When he had to sit in that wheelchair near the food court, had to endure observing all those people eating things ordinary and processed and mass produced, things that didn't even taste good. He'd been judging himself the whole time, and Shambles was judging him in a sort of merciful way and now these pictures of the naked woman with her double-mastectomy scars, yes, they were casting judgment, too. They were death carved into life and life carved into death and No Eyebrows couldn't tell where one stopped and the other started.

Shambles put her arm around him consolingly and pointed at the first picture. "She sat like this, Indian-style, all day. Letting the world see her body, her scars. She let us see her illness."

He turned to the next page. "I can't believe she's smiling."

"She was happy."

"How?"

"Will you do this for me?"

"Do what?"

"Sit naked and let me look at your body."

It was his turn to clutch the album to his chest, splayed open, protection.

"What if I do it, too?" she said, so far past her touching rule. So far past anything she'd known. The ground giving in an entirely new way.

That smile. Her smile. Almost unbeknownst to himself, No Eyebrows set the album down and stood up and took off his shirt, his socks and shoes, his pants, boxers. He stood, this frail man, in front of her, totally naked, and moved to the floor, sitting Indian-style. Eyes closed.

She stripped, too, sat across from him, maybe three feet between them, closing her eyes as well. For a long time, they didn't say anything.

"Can I open my eyes and look at you?" she asked.

"Yes."

She did (finally able to stare at him as long as she wanted!); he was smiling, a bigger one than she'd seen on his face that night in her office. "You're just as beautiful as she is."

"Describe me."

"I love the wisps of hair growing back on your head. I love your clavicles, your ribs, your cheekbones. I love that I can see so much of you. I've never seen so much of a man. I like the way your hands shake. I like that I can see your goose bumps. I love the portacath in your shoulder. It's the secret way into you, like her scars."

No Eyebrows opened his eyes and they stared at each other.

"You need to go home," she said.

"How?"

"Just go."

"I left."

"They'll understand."

"You think?" he said.

"Of course, they will."

"I don't want to die."

"No one does."

"Will you kiss me on the portacath?" he asked.

"What?"

"Please kiss me on the portacath and whisper something right into it."

And she did. Her mouth flush against it. She didn't even have to think about what to say. It was obvious.

Whispering...

Then he said, "Please hug me one more time," and so she did and during this final embrace he remembered their first hug, how much healing he'd felt that night in Damascus's bathroom. It didn't even matter if the healing wasn't real, if it had been like a sleazy minister tricking his congregation into believing he'd made the blind see, the deaf hear, the paralyzed walk. It didn't matter if the minister was fooling his parish because the audience played along, too, simulating the miraculous: men and women acting astonished as their ailments gave way to the hazy illusion of healing: eyes and ears and legs suddenly functioning, suddenly viable: they were all complicit in the parody, and somewhere inside of it, they found solace.

Because even if No Eyebrows and Shambles' hug hadn't healed him at all, even if it had been a gigantic hoax, for those few minutes he was exempt from the fatal truth.

And you must be wondering what words Shambles sent snaking up his portacath. It only seems fair for you to have all the facts.

Here goes:

"She'll forgive you," Shambles whispered.

terminal recklessness

A fresh round of misting ejaculations from the hench-men's pepper sprays kept the captives in Damascus cinching their eyes. Everyone in the makeshift prison was doing some sort of negotiation or barter with their deity, pledging to fix things about themselves they saw as character deficiencies: these ran the gamut from a woman swearing she'd never have another drop of liquor if only her god would get her out of this alive to others promising to be better spouses, better parents, better employees, better siblings, better friends, better children, better bosses. All hoping their trademarked divinity might hurl mercy if only to see these self-improvements through. Everyone was praying and begging in this fashion. Even an atheist hiding under the pool table found himself making concessions to a garbled idea of god.

Everyone in the pen except one person. Revv.

See, he was his own henchman. He was trying to open his eyes, get his bearings, despite the burning in the sockets, racking his head for a way to help Syl, a way to swing the pendulum back in their favor. He wouldn't stand by, idle and spineless.

These fascists. These censorship swine. These hooligans attacking an artist.

He'd bide his time. The tattoo said *sick with recklessness* so of course he'd help. Of course. There was no doubt about that. He wouldn't let her fight this battle on her own. This was the sort of thing that needed solidarity, even if it meant getting his ass stomped. Wouldn't be the first time or the last. But he had to be patient, with three tiers of mercenaries scouring the pen of hostages for the hero.

"There's my girl," Sam said to Syl, adjusting his goggles a bit. "I was wondering exactly who you think you are to debase these soldiers' memories."

"That's not what I'm doing."

"Not anymore," he said. "Now it's my turn to debase you."

She didn't say anything, rubbed her eyes. She'd heard the phrase "paralyzed by fear" but had never known what it meant until this second. Your body atrophied and your throat constricted. Maybe that was what people meant about life flashing before your eyes when you were dying; maybe it wasn't everything that had already happened, a pummeling summation of experiences; maybe it was a kind of clairvoyant fury over your time ending before you'd done everything you hoped to.

Oh how her high wire shook right then…

How her heart torqued…

Sam said, "We won't be chancing any antsy officers of the law. So exactly four minutes until our departure starting now, Dr. WatchDog."

"Four minutes beginning now," Dr. WatchDog called back.

"Thirty second updates."

"On the nose," said Dr. WatchDog.

"We haven't much time, my dear," Sam said to Syl, "but I think it will be an adequate allotment to accomplish our goals." He pulled a small tin of lighter fluid from his back pocket. "You may not be able to see this through your watering eyes, but it's lighter fluid. I'm going to give it to you. And you are going to squirt it on every one of your paintings. And then you're going to light them all on fire. This is what's going to happen and it's nonnegotiable."

She didn't answer.

"Hey, Santa," Sam called over to Owen.

"Yeah," Owen said.

From Dr. WatchDog: "3:30."

"Is this young lass a Smart Fucker, or is she a Stupid Fucker?" Sam said to Owen. "She's smart. Be smart, Syl," Owen said.

"Are you right-handed or left?" Sam asked Syl, but she didn't answer. "Right or left, you little bitch."

"Left," Syl whispered, wanting safety. The very safety her work mocked was what she yearned for right now. A secure distance from the unrest. She'd never thought that the storm could come to you, could change the ways the winds gusted and spiraled into your high-wire world.

"Santa, please help me convey the urgency with which I'm going to dole out the next detail. Please tell her that she has precisely five seconds to comply with my suggestion, or I'm going to light her left hand on fire. I will burn her hand off her body. You know I'm not playing so make sure she understands, okay?"

"Syl," Owen said, "just do what he wants."

"My man, Santa," Sam said. "I couldn't have phrased it better myself." He held his hand out to Syl, patting the tin of lighter fluid against her wrist so she'd know where it was, despite her aching pepper-sprayed eyes. "Well?"

She still didn't say anything, didn't move.

The pen was all quiet, with one menacing exception. Revv, biding, biding…

Byron forced his thoughts to Sky Soldiers and away from Owen. There could be no pity in a moment like this. Byron knew that.

Sam squirted the lighter fluid on her left hand. He pulled a match out, struck it. He said, "Time is of the essence, my dear, so we can't dawdle. Here's all the time you get: countdown starting now: from 5-4-3…" Sam moved the match closer to her hand, hoping she'd feel the heat and realize, truly understand that he'd do it without remorse or reconsideration. Far from it— he'd do it with satisfaction. He'd happily scar this Smart Fucker.

He'd peel the skin off her in the hopes she'd never grip a paint-brush again.

But he didn't get to complete his countdown because Revv, chock full of adrenaline and recklessness, screamed, "Might I have a moment of your time, Uncle Sam?"

Immediately, one of the henchmen (a top-tier believer in *the reason!*) began wailing on Revv, who loved every second of it. For one, he wasn't going to let this fascist light Syl's hand on fire. That was *not* going to happen. Not on his watch. Secondly, and maybe more importantly, Revv wasn't going to give Syl the op-portunity to rescind her convictions, not in front of a roomful of people who admired them. These people had all collected in Damascus because of Syl's anti-war sentiments, and what would it all mean, what would anything mean, if in the face of op-pression she desecrated her own body of work? Besides, Revv was into scarification. He enjoyed vandalizing his skin. He had those angel-wing brands on both of his shoulder blades. The guy was going to light his hand on fire. So what? A bitchin' pat-tern of scars on his hand and wrist and forearm, and he didn't even have to pay for it. Not to mention, the story itself: getting to spread rumors about the time some crazy cog from the new gestapo was going to abuse an artist and Revv saved her; think of the discordant melodies he'd yelp about his dissension! Of course it was going to hurt like hell, but he'd tolerated all kinds of punishments in the decorating of his identity—the Prince Albert piercing in his prick hurt, his tongue piercing hurt, be-ing branded hurt, the tattoos on his kidneys and chest plate and "the job-stopper" on the side of his neck hurt. But here was the point he had to stand up for: if you didn't fear consequences, you were the scariest motherfucker alive.

"Stop it," Sam said to the henchman who was still working Revv over. "Bring him here."

"He tends bar," Byron said to Sam. "Got quite a mouth on him."

"I noticed," Sam said.

"2:30," Dr. WatchDog said.

Sam shot him a vicious glower, like the elapsing seconds were the man's fault.

"You must be the hero," Sam said to Revv.

"I've never been called a hero before, Uncle Sam, but I appreciate the compliment."

"Well, you certainly fit in here, Smart Fucker. You may be smarter than our Scared Artist. Maybe you'd like to take over for her."

Revv held his left hand out for a shake. "What kind of renaissance man would I be if I refused?"

"See what I mean about the mouth?" asked Byron.

Sam punched Revv in the eye and he fell down, peered up at Sam, trying not to look worried. But the punch had surprised him. The punch made Revv regret the sarcasm; he'd have to be more alert. This wasn't going to be easy, but it wasn't supposed to be. If it was easy those sniveling idiots in the pen would be up here, too. This took something unique. You had to have a sprig of madness in you. You had to see physical pain as a puzzle. There were ways to solve it besides avoidance.

"Stand him up," Sam said to a couple mercenaries, shook his head. "I do applaud your selflessness, sir, but as I told our artist, time is of the essence. So if you will be filling in for her, I need you to take the lighter fluid and the matches and destroy these paintings."

Revv didn't say a word. The punch had made him dizzy. He'd gloriously retaliate with inaction. He would not censor Syl. He'd let this man maim him in the name of insurgency, of hope. Because you had to have hope: your hand might scar but it would heal. You'd be all right. He'd have to watch his skin sizzle and he wouldn't scream, there was no way he'd scream, he'd watch it shake and stink and rollick, and he'd look in Sam's eyes the whole time, defiant until the flames were dead.

"2:00," Dr. WatchDog said.

Revv's smile turned into a sneer.

"Told ya he was a pain in the ass," said Byron.

"Are you sure this is how you want to handle things?" Sam said to Revv.

"I think it sounds like a gas."

This was when Sam started to like Revv. He hadn't met very many heads back home who hated the homogeny of the Sane Asylum, and this kid was right up Sam's careless alley. Still, Sam had to do what he was going to do. No way around it. "You'd have made a good soldier."

"I'm not much of a morning person."

"Have it your way, Hero," Sam said to him and squirted lighter fluid all over Revv's jeans, right in his crotch, and it soaked through fast and Revv could feel the oily liquid on his cock and balls.

"What are you doing?" Revv said, bucking in the henchmen's grip.

"I'm motivating you."

"My hand. You said you were going to burn my hand."

"No, I didn't," Sam said, then asked Byron, "Did I say anything about burning his hand?"

"Not that I heard."

"You did so," Revv said.

"I said I was going to burn *her* hand." Sam punched Revv in the face again, spot on the nose this time, breaking it—a noise like somebody biting through a celery stalk ringing in Revv's ears—making his eyes tear even more, blood pouring.

One of the henchmen (a fundamentalist when it came to *the reason!*) grabbed Revv by the hair now, shaking his head around like he was a puppy. For the first time in years, Revv was scared. For the first time, despite the montage of fistfights, Revv knew he was in over his head, and there wasn't a damn thing he could do about it.

The hostages penned behind the human fence squinted their blurry eyes, trying to see the foggy scene unfurl. Not one of them felt the tug of dignity, stupidity, humility, or handicapped heroism to help Revv. They knew better. A couple even wondered why he hadn't known better.

Sam, smiling, held the unlit match in front of Revv's crotch. It was a win/win situation for Sam: the kid buckles or he doesn't. Either way, Sam and his allies were going to mutilate this place, send a cannonball smashing through the Sane Asylum's wall. "Do you want to preserve these pointless pictures, or would you like to have sex again?" Sam asked.

"Jesus, wait," Revv said.

"Seize the day, Hero."

"I can't…"

"Is there something you'd like to say?" Sam asked, still gripping the unlit match inches from Revv's crotch. "I'd make a quick decision, if I was you."

Every drop of adrenaline that Revv imagined feeding him like a superhero had run dry. He wished to be cowering in the pen with the rest of the scared people. Blend in. Assimilate. He loved Syl's art, sure, admired her undoubtedly, and was willing to indulge to a certain altitude of sadism, but not this. If the artist herself withered under the pressure, Revv could do it, too, right? No one would judge him for that, would they?

Well, would they?

"Fine," Revv said, almost whispering. "Gimme the lighter fluid." He wanted to look over at Syl, wanted there to be a moment for them to stare into each other's eyes, a fleck of understanding, some shrapnel of recognition. He had no choice here. She had to remember what he'd said that morning in bed: *your art moved me.* She'd understand. They knew each other. But when he looked over, her face was buried in her hands, shoulders heaving.

"1:00," Dr. WatchDog said.

"Hurry up," Sam said to a neutered Revv. "Shake a leg."

Revv walked from portrait to portrait, soaking them in lighter fluid.

"What about my bar?" Owen asked.

"You were given an ample opportunity to take these things down," Sam said, "but you called the cops. Now you can deal with the consequences."

Byron said to Sam, "I thought we were only going to burn the paintings."

"We are."

"But the walls will catch."

"Oops."

"Come on, man," said Byron.

"Not up for discussion, B."

"Please?" Owen begged.

"One more syllable," Sam said, "and I take that eyeball you owe me as a souvenir."

Owen looked down. Syl came over and sat next to him, resting her head on his shoulder. Nothing but that word *safety*; she wanted safety, wanted to be safe. Daphne, still barely able to see from the pepper spray, huddled with the rest of the hostages behind the human fence and was dying of shame, felt so vibrantly naïve. This was her fault. She'd crawled in Owen's ear and made him call the cops and who knew what was coming next. She remembered William asking, "Are you sure you know what you're doing?" and clearly she didn't. He was right to disregard her advice. If he wanted to get into a good college and be a "barista of the real world," the last thing he could afford was to take Daph as private counsel. Revv might have been the one using the lighter fluid and matches, but Daphne was burning her uncle's bar down. She knew so much about everything, right? All she knew now was that she was a bad niece. All in the name of art, twelve silly paintings that no one would even remember in a year's time.

"Thirty seconds," Dr. WatchDog said.

"Go," Sam said to Revv, and he struck the first match. He was a coward. Like every other disgusting American, Revv was saving himself.

He lit the first portrait on fire.

He lit the second.

He dropped the match on the floor.

He struck another.

Lit the third, fourth, fifth, sixth.

Dropped the match and struck one more.

He lit the seventh, eighth, ninth, tenth, eleventh, twelfth. He singed his fingers. He deserved it.

"Time," Dr. WatchDog said, and Revv wasn't watching, couldn't bring himself to see the portraits die. Because oil paint could only resist the extraordinary temperatures for a short time before losing the chemical tussle, the fire began erasing the soldiers' faces, their identities marred and shrouded and obliterated. Their lives expunged. The first to be defaced was Chase Anthony Turgets, whose closely shorn hair vanished, the fire working its way down his forehead and over his ears, and Jessica Kathryn Ullestad burned in the exact opposite fashion, upward—her neck, chin, mouth—her canvas going fast like a wick, as Revv had been more liberal with his use of the lighter fluid, and the other soldiers igniting and disappearing, too, Hector Escolante (who was missing an eye, thanks to Sam) was erased and Jermaine Washington was erased and John Smith and Arturo Hernandez and Maria Vasquez were erased and Brian Nguyen was erased and Dakota Williamson and Sami Habibullah and Faraji Jones and Sen-Yih Lu were all erased: each and every soldier burned up for good.

Sam said, "I want all of you to start counting aloud to sixty. Once you get to that number, you can run out of here. A couple of my men will be staying behind to make sure you don't leave the building until the count is complete. Listen to me, you will be completely safe if you leave in sixty seconds. There is nothing to worry about. The building won't burn that fast. Your belongings are in pillowcases by the front door. Start counting now."

The hostages began: "1-2-3…"

Several of the henchmen left the bar.

Sam walked over to Revv, wanted to console him, though doting on another bloke's feelings wasn't something he had much experience with. But the kid had done okay for himself. He fought back, despite being cornered, outnumbered, outgunned. That took the heart of a pit bull and Sam appreciated it. "Hey, there's no shame in wanting to use your dick again."

Revv stared at him, barren of attitude, a scolded schoolboy.

"Sometimes," Sam said, "life puts you in no-win situations."

Still nothing from admonished Revv.

"Most of life is no-win situations, kid. I'm good at them. It's written right here," and he pointed at his dog tag tattoo, USMC; Revv was glad *sick with recklessness* was hidden under his shirt. He could imagine Sam seeing it and saying that if indeed Revv was sick, it was only a common cold of recklessness, not the kind of terminal case that Sam had contracted—one with the fortitude to thrive in disaster, to love catastrophe, to prosper in mayhem. He was still pointing at USMC and said, "That says I can conquer anything."

"We have to go," Dr. WatchDog said.

"One sec," said Sam, who now turned his attention to Owen, walking up close and asking, "Don't you owe me an eyeball?"

"Please."

"Don't!" Byron Settles said to Sam, walking up close, too, the three men basically pressed together.

"What the fuck?" Sam said.

"We're out of time," Byron said. "You told us we have to get out of here at four minutes. We have to split."

"This won't take long."

"Don't put me in the middle of this," Byron said. "Because I'll do something about it."

"Will you?"

"I'll have to."

Sam and Byron squared up. Owen stuck in a terrible proximity.

"We have to leave!" a top-tier believer shouted at them.

"...31-32-33..."

"Let's just get out of here," Byron said to Sam. "You don't have to do this."

The fire growing.

Sam started laughing.

Sam saying to Owen, "You've got the strangest guardian angel in the world, Santa Claus." Then Sam walked out front of the bar, feeling alive, brutal, majestic, raw. Ready to speed away and wonder whether a clown-car full of cops would track him down. Eventually, he knew there would be consequences. If not for this then the next thing he did to transport himself. But being back already felt like a life sentence, a whole sanitized existence in the Sane Asylum. He had trouble imagining it getting much worse.

With Sam gone, it was Byron's turn to bid adieu to Owen: "I didn't want this to happen."

"What about your wife?" Owen asked.

"Told you I was a bad person."

"You saved my eye."

Owen remembered the night Byron had first said he was bad, the two of them lying under Damascus's stars. He hadn't believed him then, and Owen still didn't. Yes, Byron was in a bad way and doing a bad thing, but he stepped in when Sam was going to gouge his eyeball. That was something, wasn't it?

"I finally know what I'm made out of," Byron said, "and I don't like it one bit."

"What?"

"So many broken parts..." Byron Settles said, then he left Damascus forever.

The flames traveled up the bar's walls, reaching the ceiling, spilling across it, the patterns blazing in unspeakable colors as the mirror-shards refracted, amplified, distorted their violence. The fishing lines that held up the beer-box-clouds burned, and they fell to the floor, the sky falling, hitting some of the hostages.

Owen and Syl sat at the bar, basically catatonics. His blurry eyes taking in the destruction. Damascus was finished; everything was finished; he probably was, too. The room was so hot, people still counting. And oddly it was in this instant that Owen almost laughed. Humor was weird like that, triggered in all kinds of tactless ways. Owen sat there watching it all burn to a charred conclusion and he wanted to laugh because something so ridiculous could only happen to him. He wanted to laugh and then he was laughing. He was really laughing. Syl said, "Are you okay?" and he said, "I don't think so. No. Probably not."

The hostages were almost finished, "49-50-51," and the three remaining mercenaries took that as their cue and ran out of Damascus, hopped into waiting vehicles and sped away, and Owen looked around, the bar ablaze and he was laughing still, with hostages counting, "58-59-60," and opening their eyes, coughing, alarmed and terrified, everyone trying to help their bleary-eyed neighbors to their feet; four men carried the handcuffed police officers to safety. A few running over to retrieve the pillowcases that had everyone's belongings, then sprinting out the door and gasping fresh air.

The very first person outside had been a mortified Revv, dashing from Damascus, sprinting the six blocks to Mission Street and hailing a cab, the driver asking, "Where to?" and Revv saying, "Drive, dude. Just drive," and Revv could smell the lighter fluid soaked into his jeans and on his body and he could smell his own cowardice and he smelled worse than the dead fish, worse than anything, he was worse than anything, Revv had burned her paintings. Revv was weak, and he'd never forgive himself. That was one thing he knew for sure: this night would live on and on and he'd never be able to undo his actions, every time another indictment traveled from his brain to his heart, his heart to his brain, each time these organs gossiped back and forth.

Panicked phone calls to 911 from the staggering victims, fits of coughing, thankful to be outside of the bar.

The whole room was outlined in flames now, the walls and ceiling writhing, thrashing. The building's fire alarm began its blare.

Daphne approached Owen and said, "I'll grab the money from the register. What else do you want to save?" but he didn't answer, and she said, "Owen?" and he didn't answer, and she said, "Owen," and he didn't answer, but was still sort of giggling so Daph snatched the money from the till, came around the bar to her uncle and Syl, two statues perched on barstools. "Owen, the bar is burning down," Daphne said. "Is there anything you need to save?"

"I should have listened," Owen mumbled, not laughing anymore but its residue was on his face, a weird little grin. "Byron and me were bagel dogs..."

"Is there anything you need to save?"

"Too late."

"Tell me."

But all he could muster were the same useless syllables: "Too late."

Daphne helped her uncle and Syl make their way toward the door, and Syl looked at the skeletons of her plywood canvases, falling from the walls, some already smoldering on the floor, the soldiers erased and lying in piles with the fish bones, reduced to firewood. Unnoticeable.

Everyone was out of Damascus and on the sidewalk across the street. Flopping down and rubbing their burning eyes and wondering what the hell had just happened.

And then sirens in the distance.

"Are you injured?" Daphne said to both of them, Owen and

Syl, as they made their way across the street. They shook their heads. "Then let's all sit down over here." They joined the others who had crash-landed on the sidewalk.

The sirens growing louder.

And Revv's taxi drove to North Beach where he paid the fare and found a bar and drank whiskey. His hands were shaking. Even if he held a full shot glass up to his broken nose and breathed in whiskey's relentless scent, it wasn't enough to block out the lighter fluid. That smell would follow him for years. As would Sam's words: "Most of life is no-win situations, kid."

The bartender noticed the blood on Revv's face and asked, "What happened to you?"

"I was sitting here wondering the same thing. And I have no idea." The smell all over him.

In the melee, Owen had lost his Santa hat and beard. He watched the inferno from across the street, Syl and Daphne next to him, silent.

The megaphoned woman held the tinny machine in her hand. It seemed sad, silly, inappropriate to her. You couldn't spew theory or wishful thinking or philosophy in the midst of actual danger. There was nothing useful to say while the enemy invaded, occupied, and destroyed your home. Words were only weapons when real weapons weren't around.

Or maybe that's not true.

Or not completely true.

Here's at least some evidence to the contrary:

Because next thing you knew the Inspired Instigator did something startling: she looked at the sad, silly, inappropriate machine in her hand and you know what, she decided to say something. She decided that while they'd just been attacked and blasted with pepper spray and the paintings were gone and Damascus was burning, they, the people out on the street, were still there. Still here. They weren't gone and their voices could be heard without censorship. So she moved the tinny machine to her lips and asked everybody one simple question: "What now?"

People brought their stinging eyes up to look at her.

"This isn't the end of anything," she said. "Say it with me: 'This isn't the end of anything.'"

A few murmured along, but most people didn't. Confused. Still so scared. Heads pounding from the fumes.

"Come on," she insisted, "say it with me: 'This isn't the end of anything!'"

More people, including Daphne, spoke up this time, not with enthusiasm or verve, but given the circumstances, they were doing the best they could.

Fire trucks and ambulances and police cars closed in on Damascus and soon the next phase of this emergency would begin, none of which is important to our tale. So we can meander away from the moment with the flames finishing off Damascus, and thus finishing off Owen's bar and Revv's job and Shambles' office in one fiery swoop; meander from the people situated across the street, and the Inspired Instigator doing whatever she could to connive every hostage to yell along with her: "This isn't the end of anything! This isn't the end of anything! This isn't the end…"

And other things were happening in the world, of course. Because there always are. There has to be. A couple who'd tried for years to conceive a child finally succeeded. A son estranged from his mother for almost twenty years picked up the phone and called and apologized for his role in their corrupted history. A seventeen-year-old girl's cancer went into remission. Separated spouses decided to keep struggling through their knot of marital woes. A sunflower bloomed in Fargo, North Dakota. It rained in Orlando, Florida. A schizophrenic homeless man found a $10 bill and ate a cheeseburger and French fries and drank a Dr. Pepper. A five-month-old tried her very first bite of banana. A couple danced at their 50th wedding anniversary. All this happened as the hostages sat on the sidewalk, stupefied.

the recycling man

At approximately six a.m. on the gray morning after Damascus's burning, Owen still hadn't gone home. He sat on the curb across the street, alone, and drank malt liquor from a can. Soot and dirt were smeared all over his Santa jacket and red pants, like he'd had trouble squeezing down a tight chimney.

The sun was coming up. An elderly lady and her two Chihuahuas strolled by. One of the vultures from the Department of Parking and Traffic passed in his little golf cart, eager to help San Francisco siphon a bit of dough by ticketing citizens who were trying to sneak some unpaid time at the parking meters. A recycling truck stopped at the corner and a man got out of it to collect the big blue containers, which were stuffed with glass and plastic and paper and cardboard as well as all other sorts of paraphernalia that *didn't* belong in the recycling.

"Mind if I throw something in?" Owen said to the recycling man.

"Is it recyclable?"

"Not exactly."

"Then, yes, I mind."

Owen took off the dirty Santa jacket and held it out for the recycling man to see. "It's this."

The man pointed at a garbage can close by, only about fifteen feet down the block from Owen. "Stick it in there."

"Nah," Owen said. "That's all right. Thanks anyway."

"Tell me why."

"I promised my niece I'd get rid of it. But if I just put it in the garbage, I'll take it out again after you leave. Try and clean it up. Salvage it."

"That makes sense," the recycling man said, nodding, pondering, but not elaborating as to what about that made the least bit of sense.

This confused Owen, who couldn't think of anything to say. He still had the filthy jacket in his hand. All he wore was a thin T-shirt. Freezing.

"Ah, go ahead," the recycling man said.

Supposedly, Owen was in shock. That was what the paramedics said, and the cops, too. Much to their chagrins, Owen refused to go to the hospital.

As if it wasn't enough to endure professional meddling, Daphne concurred, though it occurred to him that if he was in shock, so was she. Daph had stayed with him for a long time after everyone left, sitting on the curb and staring at the burned bar; she tried hard to talk him into coming home with her for some rest. But he wanted time to reflect. At least that was how he'd worded it to her; however, there was very little reflection going on as he guzzled malt liquor. This was more abject fear than reflection. This was one of the most terrifying questions, another version of the question lobbed at everyone from the Inspired Instigator: *what now?*

He'd brought up this very topic with Daph before she'd left a couple hours earlier. As they sat on the curb together, he'd said, "That place was basically my home."

"It was a lot of people's homes."

"Spent more time there than in my apartment."

"Maybe it's time for a nice, long vacation," Daph said. "Once the insurance money comes through."

The surgical masks that had been stashed in the basket on

Damascus's front door were mostly lying in the gutter, every now and again one would blow a few feet away like a tumbleweed.

"Where should I go?"

"Where should *we* go."

"It's weird," he said, opening more malt liquor and setting the empty next to him on the curb; Daph passed on the invitation for another beverage. "I can't think of any place I want to go."

She broke down crying. "I forced you to call the police."

"Don't."

"I should've minded my own business."

"Promise me," Owen said, "that you'll stay in my business all the time, no matter what."

"I should've known better."

"We can't learn from someone else's mistakes," he said. "It would be a lot easier if life worked that way, but it doesn't."

"Are you mad at me?"

"We probably shouldn't vacation in Germany if people think I look like Adolf Hitler," he said, smiling.

Daph laughed, wiped her nose. Owen hugged her.

"We can go anywhere we want, right?" he said. "Where would a couple 'baristas of the world' run off to?"

"Remember my ex, Andrea. She always raved about Argentina."

"Yeah, but she was a bitch."

"I think you should decide where, since my brains got us here in the first place. You'll figure out the right spot."

Owen felt the compulsion to clarify: "My dear, I love you tons, but there's something you should know about me: the chances of me figuring anything out are low."

"That's one of the differences between us. I have faith in you."

"I know me better than you do."

"No," she said, "you absolutely do not."

Something dawned on Daph right then, and she ran across

the street to Damascus. She swiped a finger across an exposed sooty beam, blackening the tip. Then she rubbed her sooty finger above her mouth, making her own Hitler moustache.

"How do I look?" Daphne said, prancing back across the road toward him.

He couldn't see it until she got pretty close. And then he cracked up. Owen gave her a *Sieg Heil!* salute. "You look cute with it."

"Will you please get rid of that creepy Santa suit?"

"Only if you have another drink with me."

Mustached, they swallowed a couple more cans of malt liquor on the curb and kept speaking in bad German accents, then Daph tried to coax him into leaving but he waved her off— *need some time for reflection, blah, blah, blah*—and now he had the Santa jacket crumpled in his hand and was freezing his ass off and talking to the recycling man.

"So are you going to throw that thing in or what?" the recycling man said. "I'm on a schedule."

Owen cocked his arm and heaved the balled up Santa jacket into the recycling truck. He waited to feel some sort of release, freedom, a weight hauled from his pinned spirit, but nothing happened, nothing changed—he was just a guy standing on the street, shivering and baffled.

While the recycling man wheeled another big blue container to the truck, he pointed at Damascus and asked Owen, "Did you hear what happened there last night?"

"I owned the place."

"You're famous. It's all over the news this morning. A bunch of witnesses were interviewed on CNN. Some kind of riot or something, huh?"

"Did they catch them?" said Owen, but he was wondering more about Byron Settles than Sam or any of the other henchmen.

"Not yet. I bet they will. It's only a matter of time." The

recycling man hooked the big blue container to the truck; he pushed a button and the can was lifted up and over, dumping its contents. "Sounds like y'all were sure lucky."

"How am I lucky?"

"The way they're telling the story on the news, you're lucky to be alive."

Owen scoffed. "Sure."

"Seriously. It's lucky you got out of there." The bin was being lowered back to the ground, landed, and the recycling man wheeled it toward the sidewalk.

Owen finished his last sip of malt liquor, threw it in the back of the recycling truck. "I guess."

Like Byron had said, yeah, you were in one piece, one mysterious piece, all of your broken parts clanging around inside. Could you ever make something new from them? That was the problem, or as much of the problem as Owen could get his head around right then. The problem was homegrown. The problem was in his blood and capillaries and organs and plasma and skin and hair and spit.

The recycling man walked back to the truck and climbed aboard. He made a motion like he was whipping something positioned in front of the truck, honked the horn, and called to Owen as he drove away, "On Dasher and Dancer and Prancer and Vixen! On Comet and Cupid and Donner and Blitzen!"

"What are we supposed to do now?" Owen yelled.

The recycling man shrugged his shoulders. He whipped his invisible reindeer one last time. A final toot of the horn. A scream: "Remember that you're lucky to be alive!"

Part Three

(A guy goes home… free your slaves… pleading with a furious god… our tiny plywood stages… *carpe diem* and all that other rah-rah shit…)

dressing the dead

Sally's part of the story starts and ends with knockings on her front door. The first knock, the hospice nurse's. The second, the men from the mortuary retrieving her husband's body.

But, first, the nurse's, and Sally lurched to answer the door, not saying anything as she opened it.

After a few seconds, the nurse said, "Hi. Where is he?"

"In our bedroom," Sally said, noticing that the pores on the nurse's nose were huge, like seeds on a strawberry. She led him down the hallway.

"You all right?"

"I'm managing."

"Is he dressed?" the nurse said.

Sally hadn't thought of that, which, given the circumstances, seemed reasonable: "He isn't."

"He needs to be dressed."

"Why?"

"That's just how it works. I can do it, unless you'd like to."

"Um," she said. "Um…"

"You have some time to decide. The men from the mortuary won't be here for about twenty minutes. People like to do it."

"Really?"

"A way to say good-bye."

It was the word *good-bye* that hurt Sally so profoundly. "Okay," she said, "I'll dress him."

•••••••

But wait. That's not quite right. There was a knock prior

185

to the nurse's. There was No Eyebrows' knock on the door: David's knock.

His diffident creep back into their life.

The day he backtracked from his prodigal hiatus, David had sat in downtown Mill Valley, at the Depot café, on the brick patio, fighting the urge to disappear back to Damascus or any other bar and slug a pond of schnapps. He shouldn't have left, of course he shouldn't have: you don't do that. It isn't even an option. You don't skip town with a busted ego under the guise of sparing your family hardships, though he vividly remembered why he'd done it: how horrible it had been to watch his wife watch him. To watch her eyes watch his body. To watch her clean up after him. To watch her watch the oncologist's lips. To watch her wither in her own way.

And Erica... watching her face watch the violence of modern medicine firsthand. Watching her watch his conclusion. She was a breathing cue of what he'd miss.

He'd abandoned his family. He'd probably crippled any chance of reconciliation. But he'd go and ask to be let back into their house. All he could do was ask.

As a lawyer, it was difficult for David to resist the temptation to script his words, his apology. He'd been a gifted litigator, one to be reckoned with, feared for his knack of engaging disinterested jurors. This, however, wasn't a trial, and Sally wasn't a jury, so he defied the instinct to concoct a speech, walking slowly, very slowly, to their house. Where he'd defend the guiltiest person he'd ever defended.

David's body was all but finished. The headaches were intolerable. The dizziness that had at one point been intermittent now affected him all the time. The nausea. The fatigue. So forgetful.

But even the slowest walks eventually lead to where you're going. And thus, David arrived at his house. The prick in the Porsche was back.

He knocked on the door. His daughter was at school. He assumed his wife would be home alone, unless, since his vanishing, she'd altered her daily routines. He knocked, and it wasn't long before he heard her heels clacking across the terra cotta tiles.

What was left of his heart climbed up his throat. Reflexively he reached to run his fingers through his hair, raking only naked scalp.

Sally opened the door and didn't say anything, bringing her hands up and covering her mouth. Eyes wide. A gasp.

David trying to figure out where to start: "Hi." If he'd been his own client, that lone, meaningless syllable muttered by his lawyer would have been the last spoken on his behalf.

Her hands still covered her mouth. "You're alive…"

"Was that a question or a statement?"

"I'm not sure." She dropped her hands.

"Yes, I'm alive." So happy to see Sally's face: the freckles on her cheeks, smaller and darker than any he'd ever seen before, pinpricks of deep brown, like specks of coffee grounds. Those lovely, crooked teeth. Her green eyes. "I'm holding on. Barely."

"That makes two of us," she said, all her sleepless worry turning into anger. All the explanations to Erica about where Daddy was, all the lies Sally was forced to tell on his behalf, hating that he put her in the position of lying to their daughter.

Sally pushed the door open farther, an invitation, then walked toward the kitchen. He followed her into their house.

"Would you like some tea?" she said.

"Anything stronger?"

"Jesus, David, you've been drinking?"

"Stage-four," was all he said, which must have been enough of an explanation because she sighed and pulled a bottle of vodka from the freezer, mixing two vodka sodas and handing one to him. She took a sip, though they hadn't had a proper cheers. This made him think of Shambles.

"I've been drinking, too, since you left," Sally said. "I invented a cocktail: the absent husband. Vodka and a crushed Ambien in a martini glass."

Erica would say, "When is Daddy coming home?" and Sally said, "Soon," and Erica asked, "When?" and Sally said, "Soon."

"Where should I start my apology?" David said to her.

"I'm not so sure I really want an apology." Sally took a big swig from her drink. "You apologize for being later than you'd promised, or missing one of Erica's recitals, or blowing off dinner plans you and I had. If you're here to give me some insincere apology so you can die with a clean conscience, you can go to hell. I won't help you do it."

"That's not why I'm here."

"Why are you here?"

"I just said I don't know."

"Do you know when most slave owners freed their slaves?" Sally said.

"Let me—"

"On their deathbeds. Surrounded by their families." She scoffed. "Men are filthy. Filthy and dumb." Sally looked him right in the eyes and spoke in a southern drawl: "They freed their slaves on their deathbeds so they could float off to heaven. Sing 'Amazing Grace.' Angels playing harps. Loafing in the clouds. Is that what you're here to do, David? Are you here to free your slaves?"

"I thought that if you saw it, I was really dying…"

"You are really dying," Sally said.

"Can I have another?" and he handed her his empty glass. "Maybe I'll try an absent husband this time."

"Don't be charming," she said. "I can't handle any of your charm right now." She made them both fresh vodka sodas. She made these drinks stronger. She hadn't expected to see him again. Over the first couple of weeks she thought he'd grow weary, desperate, and even if his pride propped him up for a while, without his pills and treatments (she checked with Kaiser to see if he'd made/kept any appointments), Sally assumed his body would falter and, if he didn't end up back at home, she'd get a call that he was in such-and-such hospital. But days passed, weeks passed, then four months, and she stopped hoping to see him again. She stopped hoping, period.

Her explanations to Erica grew barbs: "When's Daddy coming home?" and Sally said, "He may not come home." "Why wouldn't he come home?" "I don't know, sweetie. You'd have to ask him that."

"How's Erica?" David said.

"What would your educated guess be?"

"What did you tell her?"

"She doesn't understand what's going on, and I don't have the heart to tell her the truth. I don't want her knowing what a bastard you are."

"Do you want me to leave?"

"You already left."

"Do you want me to leave now?"

"You can do whatever the hell you want."

"I'm here."

"And I'm ecstatic," she said. "Shall we eat dinner on our best china tonight? A big celebration: Daddy's home!" Sally clapped her hands sarcastically. "Daddy's home! Daddy's home!" She stopped clapping. "I'm going to take a nap."

"What should I do?" David said.

Sally didn't answer.

He stood in the hollow kitchen, listening as she slammed the bedroom door.

••••••••

David snuck into the master bathroom while she napped. Tiptoed by her. She still wore the same eye mask to sleep.

He opened his medicine cabinet. There were his hair products. All of them. An entire shelf. Styling gel, leave-in conditioner, waxes, molds, a couple kinds of pomade.

He picked up the leave-in conditioner; he picked it up and unscrewed the cap; picked it up and unscrewed the cap and squirted a huge meringue into his palm and rubbed it all over his hairless head. He stood looking at himself in the mirror, scalp covered in what looked like ranch dressing.

Stood looking and thought: what have I done?

········

"I'm going to pick Erica up," Sally said, three hours later.

Three hours of David sitting in the barren kitchen after he swabbed his head clean. Three hours of a devastating silence in which he had to admit that he might have accomplished his ultimate goal: Sally wouldn't remember his deterioration or death, even if he lay in their bed for months, cells slowly parceling his body into oblivion: all she'd remember was that he'd left them: he'd left and that would be his legacy.

"Can I come with you?" he said.

"Might as well get the family reunion over with."

········

A scene from the awkward car ride: David saying, "Should we tell her the truth?"

Sally laughing. Laughing hard.

"What's so funny?" he said.

"What's the truth?"

"About where I've been."

"She thinks you were having tests. No sense telling her any different. I wish that was what I thought you were doing."

"What do you think I was doing?"

"Go to hell," she said.

········

"Daddy!" Erica said. "How were your tests?"

The guilt and shame he'd felt first seeing Sally flew into a vulgar orbit. His only child was here smiling and running toward him and how did he think it a good idea to spend a day away from this? Not only was she running toward him with that smile, but she wore her red tap shoes, clacking loudly with each step.

The red tap shoes she'd lived in for the last year or so, ever since she began taking tap dancing classes. In fact, these were her second pair, as she'd worn through the first, refusing to take them off regardless of where she was.

"My tests were great. How's my baby doll?" He got out of the car's passenger seat and tried to pick her up. He couldn't. He kneeled in front of her, and they hugged. "Still wearing your fancy shoes, I see."

"I'm getting very good. I'll give you a show at home."

"I can't wait."

"My teacher says my tap shoes are too loud in class."

"What does she know?"

"Get in the car, you two," Sally said. "We're holding up traffic."

David stood up and looked behind them, not a car within fifty feet. He helped his daughter into the backseat and buckled her in.

········

Sally and David sat on the couch watching their daughter dance on a piece of plywood that had been cut into a rectangle, a small stage for her to practice on. She tapped, tapped away, clumsy little steps in her thunderous red shoes. She had a huge smile on her face. She finished her routine and asked, "How was I?"

"Perfect," David said.

"Great," Sally said.

Erica ran over and pulled her parents into a family hug. Sally tried not to touch him.

········

They ordered a pizza and sat at the kitchen table. The conversation revolved around Erica. It had to. Sally couldn't look at him.

"Would you like another piece, baby doll?" David said to his daughter.

She nodded. "I love pizza."

"I know you do."

"Are you going away again for more tests?" Erica said.

"I'm not going anywhere."

Finally, Sally looked at David.

•••••••

They tucked her in bed and went back into the kitchen and David was ready for a battle. Ready for Sally to scream in his face and call him an asshole and threaten to call the police if he didn't get out of their house.

But all that happened was that she shook drinks in a martini shaker, poured them into glasses. "I'm assuming this is your first absent husband," she said.

"It is. Let's make a toast."

"Let's not."

"Not a serious one," he said. "Something silly. How about this: *to livers aching like shin splints?*"

"Are you a poet now?"

He didn't say anything. Their glasses touched. Then they took sips.

"I don't want to know anything about where you've been," she said. "Not one word."

"Okay."

"You're a son of a bitch."

"I know."

No words from either of them for quite a while, until he said, "I don't really like my absent husband. The pill makes it bitter."

"I don't really like mine either," Sally said.

•••••••

So first David knocked and then it was the nurse's turn. Sally showed the nurse down the hall to their bedroom. To David's body. The nurse confirmed that he was dead and said, "You have about fifteen minutes to get him dressed. Do you want help?"

"I can manage," Sally said.

Sally didn't really want to do it, didn't want to dress this man who had abandoned them. She looked at her husband, lying there, his mouth open, the last tentacles of spit leaking out its corners. A huge purple cold sore in the middle of his bottom lip.

"Does it matter what he wears?" Sally said.

"Whatever you want."

"Is it cold outside?"

The nurse didn't answer.

"I'm sorry," she said. "That was silly."

The nurse touched her forearm. "No, it wasn't." He took a few steps back to give her space, unless she asked for his help.

It was all David had talked about, when he could still talk, before the tumor in his brain confiscated his ability to talk, to see, to stand. Sure, the nurse knew how cold *other* people could get from chemo, but the nurse didn't hear David's raspy voice asking her for one more blanket before his voice inexplicably shut off one afternoon; Sally asking him questions and him staring at her with confused, scared eyes and her saying, "Say something," but he never uttered another word. The nurse didn't know that Sally sat on the edge of the bed and fondled his earlobes while he slept and called them frozen grapes.

David had been naked since the morphine patches. No longer able to swallow pills, aspirating them, almost choking to death. Sally put the patches on his back and they pumped a steady stream into him, dulling the pain, dulling everything. He slept all day, his body drawing on the last of its water stores, from the kidneys. He was no longer cold and Sally saw no reason to keep changing his clothes every time he soiled the bed, no reason to put either of them through that wretched choreography. And so she'd sit next to his naked body, sometimes lie next to him, her hand rubbing his earlobes. She'd exist in all that silence. All the final, nurturing words unspoken and trapped in his cragged lungs. It wasn't supposed to end without a good-bye. And no matter how much she loathed the notion, couldn't she be the last slave he freed from his deathbed?

"I can dress him, if it's too hard," the nurse said.

"I'll manage," Sally said, going to the closet and grabbing his black sweater, a pair of jeans, black socks. She pulled the covers back, his body deflated from one hundred eighty pounds to one-twenty.

When he'd first come back she hadn't sat on the bed with him. That was too close. At first, she sat in the wheelchair, positioned adjacent to the bed. She sat in it and wondered where he'd run away to. She could imagine the sordid details of his adventure and didn't need the actual rendition; the particulars were meaningless. He'd left. Period. Period, he'd left and whether or not he cried himself to sleep every night with alienation and misery and self-disgust (she doubted it), it didn't change the simple fact he'd deserted them. The problem for Sally was that the argument didn't end there. He'd left and she was beyond angry—she was under some brawn of anger that she'd never known before—yet her love for him kept growing, like a corpse's fingernails. It was sick. She should have stayed mad. She should have loved him less every second.

Sally sat in the wheelchair, still warming up to him, to his being home again. It was the wheelchair that made Sally send Erica away for the final days of his dying. It was when Sally saw Erica leap into the wheelchair and yell, "I've got big tumors, too!"

"Don't do that," Sally said.

"I've got tumors, Mommy."

"Get out of it."

"But I've—"

And Sally slapped her. Twice. She slapped Erica twice in the face, before gaining control, crying, apologizing, and sending her daughter to stay with Sally's sister in Seattle, until this was over.

Sally had begged him: say good-bye to Erica. "Tell your daughter you love her and live a great life."

"I can't say those things," he whispered.

"You're dying, David."

But all he said was, "I'm not dead yet."

"She needs to hear you say good-bye," Sally said, speaking not only on her daughter's behalf, but on her own; Sally needed to hear the same thing, you selfish dying man. Why would you want to deprive your family of something so basic?

For weeks after his death, Sally went through his things in the hopes of finding a mysterious letter: a note conveying sentiments that were too hard for him to verbalize. Words of devotion, words that validated their marriage, their family. But she found nothing.

In a sense he still showed his selfishness, posthumously—each new place Sally ransacked in the hopes of finding his furtive correspondence only exacerbated her anger. There was no good-bye. He hadn't written them anything.

Sally started with the jeans. Holding one of David's legs up at the calf, working the stiff material over his foot and ankle; she did the same thing with the other leg. She moved her hands up to his thigh, continued shimmying the jeans, and what was she supposed to do with the hips, how was she supposed to hoist his weight to get the pants pulled up, and she slapped her daughter twice, and the nurse asked, "Do you want help?" and Sally said, "No, I can manage," and she rocked her husband from side to side, struggling to yank the denim high enough. Earlobes frigid as frozen grapes, and the jeans kept slipping out of her hands, and she hoped she could do it, and the jeans kept slipping, and the nurse said, "Are you sure?" and Sally said, "I can manage," but it was only getting harder and she knew she'd never be able to do it by herself and her breathing sped up and she turned away from her husband and shoved his wheelchair over. Kicked it. Couldn't wait until it was out of their house. Couldn't wait until she spackled the spots in the paint that had been scuffed by her wild driving of this machine, the times she smashed his feet taking corners too quickly. The way he'd grimace and try not to complain. The way she'd grimace, too, standing behind his back.

And there were other things happening in the world, of course, because our lives all spin on the same spit. Seconds and heartbeats don't stop until the clockwork breaks and the arteries dam... Syl prepared for a new installation at a Chelsea gallery; the news of her art and the violence it incited (and the media coverage) had made greedy gallery curators fawn for the follow-up, themed around war again: this time, Afghanistan; the featured metaphor would be spider webs: the way Iraq was merely one strand of the spider's silk, one thread in a despicable grid of imperialism that stretched into America's past and also the future of a rotting empire, one that stank worse than Syl's dead fish.

Syl was trying to funnel the fear she'd experienced that night at Damascus straight back into her artwork. One thing she'd definitely learned from this entire wonder/debacle was that art could, as Revv so poetically put it, *stir shit.*

People often asked her if she regretted using actual soldiers' portraits in the Olfactory Installation, was she perhaps wrong in her appropriation of their faces, was it demeaning, disrespectful, too much? Yeah, we lived in a remix culture but had she crossed a line? And would she have done things differently knowing then what she now knew?

"It's still too close," she'd say. "Ask me in a decade."

"But were you in the wrong?" some persisted.

"I wasn't totally in the right. Is there a third choice?"

Meanwhile, a plastic surgeon in downtown San Francisco had been consulted about the removal of Owen's birthmark. A day had been chosen. A time. The procedure went off without a hitch (god love insurance money). He healed normally. No scarring. Sure, in a perfect scenario, he wouldn't have needed its removal to see himself more positively: on a planet nude of human insecurities, he would have realized that the birthmark didn't define his identity; he'd have found a bastion of inner strength and accepted himself, birthmark and all. Agreed: that would be a better story. But that wasn't what happened, and this isn't revisionist history.

He and Daph were still planning a long vacation. Decided on spending five weeks in New Zealand and leaving soon. They had to wait until she finished getting her teaching credential. Besides, that gave them something to celebrate. Rather than a sojourn with confusing implications—what was Owen supposed to do with his life now that the bar was gone?—they could focus their attention on the known: Daph was going to get in the classroom and help kids, which was something they both felt great about.

Revv was in San Diego. Revv was a guilty, embarrassed mess. It had been months since the incident, and he felt displaced and lonely and his heart was squalid, and he hadn't been sober the whole time because he couldn't handle hearing his mind arraign his cowardice. He had no alibi, no legitimate defense, and quickly, the verdict was issued and the punishment severe: Revv was to heat a knife over an open flame and hold it to his arm, obfuscating *sick with recklessness* underneath a sloppy, homemade scar.

He'd spent time in San Diego before and was hanging out with the same heads. These people knew he had been branded—those functionless angel wings on his shoulder blades. So they asked him about the new scar on his bicep. It was fresh and colorful and sort of shaped like California.

"What's the scar represent?" they'd say.

How he hated the vandalism he'd masterminded all over his body. If he could erase every image and bragging word and close every pierced hole, he would do it. If only he could shed his skin like the Bowie Constrictor and start over with pristine flesh.

This time, he'd mar it with only one word: coward.

He had called Owen once since bolting town, and Owen said, "Well, I guess you're fired."

"Guess so. I don't know what to say."

"You didn't have a choice, kid. Don't worry about it."

"How's Syl?"

"She's recovering. You should call her."

"She must think I'm a total pussy."

"You kidding? She thinks you're Ghandi. What you did was amazing. Retarded, but amazing."

"I can't call her, but tell her I really liked hanging out with her."

"Will do. One more thing?" Owen said. "Then I'll leave you alone for the rest of your life."

"What?"

"Don't turn into me."

These were normally the moments when Revv vomited a one-liner. But all he said this time was, "I'll try."

You know what Byron Settles did? He went skydiving. Not for a few years still. For a few years, he had to pay the price for what had happened at Damascus. He got sober in prison, attended AA meetings. Actually, skydiving was his sponsor's idea: "Might help you move on to go back to the scene of the real crime. In your case, that's the sky." The sponsor set it up through one of the outfits that used tandem jumping, in which you were hitched to someone more experienced than you. Of course, Byron had hundreds of hours more than the guy he was tethered to, but that wasn't the point. The point was jumping out of the plane again, freefalling, feeling the jerk as the shoot opened and you drifted down. "You ready to rumble?" the guy had asked right before they leaped from the plane, and Byron said, "I've been rumbling. I'm ready to go home." His knee was fine on the landing.

Shambles was thinking a lot about No Eyebrows, assumed his wife had taken him back, since he'd never returned to her apartment. Not a day went by that Shambles didn't wonder if this was the day he had left his life.

Shambles had seen the burned bar early the morning after its destruction. (Actually, she'd just missed Owen and the recycling man by a few minutes.) She was on her way to an Irish pub up on Valencia Street that catered to the early-bird drinkers—not just the all-day drunks, but commuters stopping in for a quick martini to veil their shaking hands from their bosses. For Shambles, if there was ever a time to drink whiskey in the a.m. surely this was it: hours removed from sending No Eyebrows home, relentless hours alone in her apartment, pensive and uneasy with the roar of nocturnal second guessing. *What had she done? Why had she done it? Was it even the right thing to do?* It was almost like she was seasick.

So she decided to get out of her house, take a walk, enjoy the morning, indulge in a couple rounds at the pub. Clear her head, cloud her head, what was the difference? And that was when she saw Damascus. Or what was left of it. Looking bombed out. The wreckage. Everything around it was fine. That was the detail Shambles fixed on: everything else was the same: all around the bar, there were no signs of calamity. Normal storefronts and restaurants. Apartment buildings unblemished.

She used to watch *The Andy Griffith Show* when she was a kid. Otis, the town drunk, with the approval of the local police, used to lock himself in a jail cell every night he needed to sleep one off, to save himself from any more drama or public humiliation. What would he have done if the sheriff's office had burned down, she wondered, much like Damascus, her own office? How do you go back out into the wild when you were used to keeping yourself in a cage?

········

Now Sally said to the nurse, "How am I supposed to do this?" and the nurse walked over and turned the wheelchair upright and said, "Let me help you."

They lifted David's hips and slipped on the jeans. The nurse didn't know how cold he'd been, and together they pulled the sweater over his head, over that purple cold sore, but navigating the sweater's sleeves wasn't as easy, taking a lot of time to slide the arms through, because the dead weight was topsy-turvy; they came up with a solution: one at a time, the nurse propped David's arms up from under the sweater, while Sally reached for his wrists and guided them through the sleeves.

Sally put socks on him and said, "Shoes?" but the nurse shook his head no. I've got big tumors, too, and Sally asked the nurse to go in another room. So she could say good-bye. To him. And he wouldn't answer.

"I'll wait in the hall," the nurse said.

But Sally didn't do any talking. He hadn't said any words in over a week. Sally noticed the veins in his face that were leeching to the skin's surface. Examining that huge purple cold sore. She fondled the freezing grapes, and she hoped the men from the mortuary would get lost. That they'd take a wrong turn and not find the house. End up knocking on some other woman's door, asking for her husband's corpse, and twice Sally smacked Erica, and after she'd hit her, Sally saw her daughter's hands come up to protect her face. Sally said, "Stop it," and Erica said, "You stop it," and Sally collapsed, she surrendered and gasped, the two of them crouching, falling to their knees at the feet of that terrible wheelchair like they were praying, pleading with a furious god.

Lying next to him for the last time, Sally wondered if she could ask the nurse to go home; she could say, "I'll manage," and she could turn off the lights and lock every door. Before the third and final knock. Before the mortuary men slammed their knuckles into the wood.

Knocking...

Yes, knocking...

Before the edges of the world folded over her like a crepe.

our tiny plywood stages

First thing we notice is the noise, tap shoes clomping out a clumsy rhythm. This is accompanied by excessive breathing, panting really, as the little girl currently wearing those red tap shoes has been performing for fifteen minutes straight and she is winded. In all honesty, she is exhausted, but she's entertaining her mother and she will not stop. She is trying to cheer her mother up. She is swinging her arms and smiling hugely and she knows it is working. The girl is convinced of this, and the dancing will continue until she's satisfied that the mother's mood has been mended, at least until tomorrow's performance.

"Look at me go!" Erica says.

The shows happen daily now.

Sally sits on the couch and watches her daughter stomp on her tiny plywood stage. It's an early evening recital. And the daughter is right in her theory that the dancing cheers the mother up. It does. There's something naked about it. Something simple. And if there's one thing Sally has learned since David died it's that life is rarely simple, so when it is, when there's a respite from the demands and aches and harsh routines of adult commitments, immerse yourself in that moment, enjoy its amnesia because it won't last long.

So we watch as Sally relishes the show: the only things in the whole world that matter to her are Erica's feet in the red shoes clacking on the plywood. There are other things happening out there, sure, but for Sally and Erica, there's just this.

"Look at me go!" Erica says, still dancing, her feet stomping away on her tiny plywood stage, her arms flailing, huge smile on her face.

beginner's luck

Shambles didn't want to drink. Not here. Not at this place. Not in a god damn comedy club. But Shambles' ex-husband had asked her very nicely: "It would mean a lot to me if you were there. It's only an open mic night, but it's my first time performing on stage. Please? I need all the help I can get." She'd have refused if it hadn't been for that last line—*I need all the help I can get.* Lately, Shambles was of the opinion that this was the only thing we should ever say to one another.

It was a rainy Monday and Shambles had nothing to do anyway, so she schlepped across town to North Beach and ordered a Coke from the bartender, which made her feel sort of silly, a grown woman drinking soda in a bar. She tipped him five dollars because she hadn't ordered alcohol, a guilty tithe.

The room was pretty empty, maybe ten people total. The stage looked cheap, barely raised off the floor. Shambles assumed most of the people in the audience were like her—family, ex-family, friends unable to wiggle out of coming to support these aspiring comedians. No one wanted to be here, she was sure of that. No one wanted to listen to beginners, amateur jokesters cutting their teeth, taking their lumps, finding their hilarious ways in the world.

She sat at a small, round table intended for two people. Soon, her ex-husband approached and stood in front of her. He was wearing a suit. He looked really nice. Younger, even. That was the first thought that registered: he looked younger, and she looked... well, not younger.

"Irene, you made it," her ex said.

She hadn't identified with that name in a long time. "I did. Just barely."

"Can I buy you a drink? They gave me two free drink tickets."

"I've got this." She jiggled her soda. "Nervous?"

"I am."

"You'll be fine. You've always loved jokes."

"If you're any indication, I don't think anyone will think I'm funny."

"I think you're funny," she said.

"That's not how I remember things."

"How do you remember things?"

"Differently than you do," he said. "I think that was one of our problems."

"When do you go on?" Irene asked and finished her Coke.

"Here." He set his two drink tickets on the table. "Just in case you need any alcohol to enhance my punch lines. I wasn't sure you'd show up."

"It's the least I can do."

"No, the least would have been blowing me off," he said. "This is the second least thing."

She laughed. "See? You're funny sometimes."

"I heard about Damascus. Thank god you weren't there for the fire."

"What a weird story..." she said and paused, planned on elaborating because it was much more than merely peculiar. It was a tragedy. It had changed her life. Or she thought it had changed her life. She wasn't sure yet. But Irene didn't get the opportunity to talk more because everyone's attention suddenly turned to the tiny stage.

A woman with huge boobs ambled onto it, boobs wedged

into her blouse so the tips of them curved down like toucan beaks. "Good evening, all you gutter-balls and train-wrecks," she said. "How goes it? What's the matter? How many lies have you told yourself today?"

She left a crevasse of time here for the crowd to laugh, which it did sympathetically and unenthusiastically.

"Welcome to 'Beginner's Luck,'" she continued, "the longest running open mic comedy night in San Francisco. We'll be getting started in just a couple minutes, so grab another drink and settle in for what I hope will be so funny you'll think nitrous oxide is seeping through the vents… thanks." She walked offstage.

"She's hysterical," her ex said.

"I guess."

"I better get ready to go on. Thanks again for being here."

"Break a leg."

"From you, dearest, that sounds vaguely threatening."

"It vaguely was," she said. "Are you going to make fun of me in your set?"

"I'm going to make fun of us a bit, our marriage. But not you."

"Don't point me out to the rest of the crowd."

"Of course not."

"I don't want people to know it's me they're laughing at."

"I wouldn't do that."

Irene didn't really believe him. It didn't matter, she guessed, if he flung jokes about how dim-witted she was, what a crappy wife she'd been, how in the midst of hoping for a different life she forgot to live her own. At least she had his drink tickets. Maybe all his jokes would be funny if she broke her prohibition and had some free whiskey. Maybe laughing at herself would feel good.

If that was the case, however, if laughing at her decisions would truly help, then she should be the one to mount the stage and tell jokes. In doing so she could stake claim to her story, plant a flag in it, like the marines at Iwo Jima; call out what it truly was: a mess... *my life's a mess.*

The MC mounted the small stage again and said, "Before I close sign-ups for tonight's show, are there any last-minute performers? Anybody just find the gumption to get up here and try?"

The fingers on Irene's right hand tingled, her forearm, the sensation moving toward her shoulder, like a fever sprawling. Her arm wanted to rise. Wanted her whole body to find the courage and follow suit.

The MC continued her sales pitch to the modest audience: "The show must go on, folks, so it might as well go on with you. It ain't as easy as it looks, that I can guarantee, but trust me on this: it's better to be heckled than to be invisible, better to spin the wheel and play the game than watch from the sidelines. So *carpe diem* and all that other rah-rah shit... any courageous souls out there want to get up and give it a shot?"

An arm ascending...

Also published by **TWO DOLLAR RADIO**

THE ORANGE EATS CREEPS
A NOVEL BY GRACE KRILANOVICH
A Trade Paperback Original; 978-0-9820151-8-6; $16 US
* National Book Foundation 2010 '5 Under 35' Selection.
* *NPR* Best Books of 2010.
* *The Believer* Book Award Finalist.

"Krilanovich's work will make you believe that new ways of storytelling are still emerging from the margins." —*NPR*

THE CORRESPONDENCE ARTIST
A NOVEL BY BARBARA BROWNING
A Trade Paperback Original; 978-0-9820151-9-3; $16 US

"A deft look at modern life that's both witty and devastating."
—*Nylon*

"Intelligent... a pleasure to read."
—*Bookslut*

THE PEOPLE WHO WATCHED HER PASS BY
A NOVEL BY SCOTT BRADFIELD
A Trade Paperback Original; 978-0-9820151-5-5; $14.50 US

"Challenging [and] original... A billowy adventure of a book. In a book that supplies few answers, Bradfield's lavish eloquence is the presiding constant."
—*New York Times Book Review*

THE VISITING SUIT
A NOVEL BY XIAODA XIAO
A Trade Paperback Original; 978-0-9820151-7-9; $16.50 US
"[Xiao] recount[s] his struggle in sometimes unexpectedly lovely detail. Against great odds, in the grimmest of settings, he manages to find good in the darkness."
—Lori Soderlind, *New York Times Book Review*